Publish and be damned
www.pabd.com

Dear Pete

Mrs Moneypenny: E-mail from Tokyo

Heather McGregor

*Enjoy !
These are the first
8 months of the
column

HBM
XII·07*

Publish and be damned
www.pabd.com

First published in Great Britain 2005 by Heather McGregor.
The moral right of Heather McGregor to be identified as the author of this work has been asserted.

Designed in London, Great Britain, by Adlibbed Limited.
Printed and bound in the UK by 4Edge.

ISBN: 1-905452-40-3

To Jackie Shorey,
an outstanding editor and
an even better friend.

CONTENTS

ACKNOWLEDGEMENTS

The original Mrs Moneypenny columns would never have appeared without the help and encouragement of the staff and readers of The Business, the magazine published with the Weekend Financial Times from October 2ⁿᵈ, 1999 until its demise in July 2002. Mrs Moneypenny's weekly contributions – literally by e-mail from Tokyo – were commissioned, edited, debated and commented on by all of them.

This book would never have appeared without the almost single-handed work of Anne Heining, who compiled and edited the copy, chose the photographs and kept me on track to finish the project. For this she is owed the most enormous vote of thanks. While all the errors and omissions are mine, none of them would have made it on to the page without her.

Heather McGregor
November 2005

INTRODUCTION

Seven months pregnant and without a word of Japanese. That's how I arrived in Tokyo to take up my new job in October 1998. The job itself was pretty undefined, at least in the eyes of the American I had notionally come to work for. Our only previous meeting had been a couple of weeks earlier at breakfast in a London hotel. Now I was sitting in front of him getting my instructions. He had an office that was large and also largely empty. The desk was immaculate. "So", he said, "what can you do?"

What I could do, as it turned out, was run the office very efficiently on his behalf. Looking back on the whole experience, I am amazed that I dared to roll up my sleeves and get stuck in to the day to day business of an investment bank in Tokyo. But at the time, I was quite clearly suffering from delusions brought on no doubt by the raging hormones of my advanced state of pregnancy. I readily agreed to tackle his problems one at a time until they were all resolved.

We couldn't have been more different. I was an over-educated Protestant girl in her late thirties who was the product of a comfortable middle-class upbringing. He came from a poor Catholic Irish family who had settled in Boston a generation before his birth, and he had missed out on the whole further education experience. He used to joke with me that I wouldn't be the only MBA in the office; my MBA had been obtained through hard grind in the lecture theatres and library of the London Business School, whereas the others were simply Married But Available.

The real reasons behind my arrival in Tokyo, and more specifically his office, were a bit (but not much) more thought out than they appear at first. Mr. M, fed up with his job in Singapore working for a vast media empire, had agreed to set up a Japanese office for that selfsame empire. I had always loved Japan, had been there regularly over the years on business, and adored Japanese food. I was working in Singapore too, but the combination of the end of my assignment and the imminent arrival of our third child had led me to seek a sabbatical from The Bank, which I planned to spend quietly in Japan working on my long overdue PhD thesis. However, this was not to be. The Bank had recently promoted one of my favourite managers to the stratosphere and given him its worldwide

13

equities business to develop. In the first month of my sabbatical, this demi-god put it to me that as I was going to be in Japan anyway, why didn't I spend a few days a week helping the newly installed American get things under control.

Things needed to be under control. October 1999 was only a year away, and there was much to do. On that date Japan was scheduled to have its own Big Bang. For those of you too young or too ignorant of the ways of the Square Mile, this was an event that took place in the UK in 1986 and in the USA in 1978. Despite Japan being built on a major fault line (see chapter on disasters), the term Big Bang did not refer to a seismic incident but the ending of fixed commissions in a financial marketplace. Up until that date, every investor, be he (or she) small or large, an individual or an institution, all paid the same commission for buying and selling stocks and shares. In Japan there was a scale of charges according to size, but the average commission paid for onshore transactions stood at more than 100 basis points, bank speak for more than one per cent. This compared, in 1998, to less than one fifth of that charge paid by fund managers in Europe or the US. While our little operation was steadily growing its revenue, it was clear that four-fifths of it was likely to disappear overnight in a year's time.

Two things were going to happen as a consequence of Big Bang. One was that many small stockbrokers would go to the wall as the margins in the business disappeared. The other was that many foreign investors who had previously settled their share-buying transactions offshore to avoid the high charges would now move onshore and probably set up operations there. Both of these dynamics would change the face of stockbroking in Japan forever. And I was going to be there when it happened.

OCTOBER 2ND, 1999
SCOUT BADGES OPEN DOORS IN TOKYO

It's official. Japan is out of recession. As a working mother of three living in Tokyo I am hopeful this will have a direct effect on my next bonus. My boss at The Bank tells me anyone could have forecast gross domestic product would have shown positive growth in two successive quarters. His economic indicators are the time it takes to find a parking space at the local shopping centre and the number of people buying new cars in his suburb. On the basis of these objective measures he invested most of his last year's bonus in a Japanese fund; other than buying shares in something.com I doubt he could have made a better decision. I shall have to follow suit – better late than never.

The only reason I have any money to invest is that we finally sold our house in London. The transaction had its moments, not least when the prospective purchaser (an investment analyst) found himself in the middle of a "European bank meets US bank meets failed UK broker" collision, and e-mailed me to see if there were any jobs going at our office in the UK. While I could see the merits of recommending him, I didn't feel that I would be seen as an unbiased reference. Fortunately he received a large payoff and we duly completed. It must have been substantial because he then disappeared on a two-month holiday. My husband now thinks we accepted too little money. I assure him that any underpricing will be more than compensated by the imminent performance of our new Japan Tracking Fund.

Of course our purchaser should have moved to Japan where the shortage of investment analysts even made a headline in the FT last month. Several friends are at home in Tokyo enjoying what is referred to in the UK as "gardening leave". The phrase does not translate well. With the possible exception of Bill Gates, it is hard to think of anyone who could afford a house with a garden here. Even if our Japan Tracking Fund returns 100 per cent I cannot see us ever moving from our bijou residence in Minami Aoyana. While palatial by Japanese standards, it is bordered on three sides by neighbours whose windows I can lean over to close if it starts to rain. All for a bargain £6,250 per month.

Importing people from overseas is not necessarily a solution to the tight labour market, as I am busy finding out. The Japanese have a lot of respect for pieces of paper, such as exam certificates, and find it hard to believe that any organisation would pay millions of yen to lure someone who left school at sixteen, let alone relocate them plus wife, nanny, children and a 40-foot container from somewhere more than 6,000 miles away. I have spent many hours patiently explaining that precisely this sort of person is best suited to trading Japanese stocks. However, I feel that not much progress is being made. I am going to make it compulsory for all prospective employees to have at least three impressive pieces of paper when they move to Japan. Boy Scout knot-tying certificates will be fine.

My husband possesses few academic qualifications. His suggestion to the agent handling his visa application last year that they add my qualifications to his and average them out met with an icy stare. As everyone is referred to by surname in Japan, I offered to lend him my MBA certificate but the agent wasn't fooled. In the end, letters from TV proprietors around the world persuaded the government to issue a visa in proportion to his seniority. Given that the class of visa is key to the availability of childcare (only expatriates with very senior jobs are legally allowed to sponsor immigrant domestic help), and we have three children, we all breathed a sigh of relief. Even in the tightest labour market, I couldn't see myself persuading The Bank to start a crèche.

OCTOBER 9TH, 1999
DANGER FOR THE NUCLEAR FAMILY
Nikkei 225: 18,062

Turkey, Taiwan and now Tokyo. We were expecting an earthquake, not a nuclear accident. The first we heard of it was a telephone call from my father-in-law in Sydney at 7am, where it was the main news story of the day. After establishing that (a) the incident had taken place more than 150km from central Tokyo and (b) the problems with Chernobyl occurred within a radius of 30km, I set off for work. I have seen enough episodes of *The Simpsons* to know what effects a nuclear accident can have.

The government blamed the lack of immediate information on the fact the offending plant was privately owned, but at least showed its concern by deferring a planned cabinet reshuffle. By lunchtime, CNN had whipped Tokyo's expatriate population into such a frenzy that apparently the afternoon flights to Okinawa were full of women and children heading for neutron-free zones. When out running (well, walking faster than usual) with my personal trainer that morning, his question: "Are you glowing yet?" took on a whole new meaning.

I have employed the services of a personal trainer in an attempt to move closer to the "Elle Macpherson" than the "Dawn French" silhouette. Bruce is Canadian, 42, drop-dead gorgeous and (apparently) heterosexual; just the sort of person I don't want to see me in my shorts. Of course, if I could shed 15 years as well as 15 kg I might be able to secure a job in one of the many hostess bars that abound in Tokyo, and earn rather more per hour than I do at present.

Roppongi, the area of central Tokyo that caters mainly to the nightlife needs of foreigners ("gaijin"), sports more than its fair share of lap-dancing clubs and, despite never having visited one, the economics of these places never ceases to fascinate me. It costs ¥7,000 (£40) to enter and that includes two drinks; lap dances themselves are a further ¥7,000. Cash is acceptable or one can buy books of eight "dance tickets" by credit card. All this, of course, distracts the client from noticing that he is being charged ¥1,200 (£6.50) a beer. I remarked to my boss the other day that a lap-dancing club would make a great MBA case study. He said such places were usually full of MBAs – men who were Married But Available. Personally, I doubt many expat managers get closer to these places than signing expense receipts, and as these are in Japanese anyway, they would probably never notice.

Another service readily available in Tokyo is the humble taxi. It is the rainy season and I had feared that taxis in Japan, like Hong Kong and Singapore, were water-soluble. Discovering that this is not the case was a great relief. Mind you, the minimum fare is ¥660 (£3.75) and I have to try not to think about the fact that I could take the famiiy for a week in Antigua for the money I have spent on taxis this year.

Unlike taxis, good and affordable staff in the banking sector remain scarce. Having successfully persuaded the immigration authorities that Boy Scout knot-tying certificates demonstrate a candidate's strong suitability to trade Japanese shares, I now look like being thwarted by the regulators in my attempt to use imported labour.

Originally, I had been encouraged by the fact that, for the first time, one of the regulatory authorities is setting its exam in English. As there are four Japanese alphabets, this move was very promising. But my joy has been mitigated by hearing that the set text for the exam retails at a cool ¥1m (£5,700), which would buy 143 lap dances or 100 hours with Bruce "The Body". Think how thin I would be then.

OCTOBER 16ᵀᴴ, 1999
FREE CIGARETTES, A PERK FOR THE ELDERLY
Nikkei 225: 17,601

My husband has told me that he thinks ¥1.9m (£10,700) is too much to pay for a handbag. There are obviously a lot of Japanese who do not agree with him. As the country crawls out of recession, the waiting list for the ultimate trophy handbag, Hermès' Kelly Bag, has lengthened to almost five years.

The Hermès shop informs me that prices for the bag range from ¥500,000 to ¥1.9m, depending on the leather and stitching requested. Each bag is made to order, hence the wait. Of course, if I wanted to, I could always go to one of the many second-hand shops in Tokyo that act as a clearing-house for unwanted designer items. I dropped into one such shop yesterday and had a good look at the 20 Kelly Bags in stock. The price tags ranged from ¥800,000 to ¥3m, such is the premium that Japanese ladies are prepared to pay for instant gratification.

Not many Kelly Bags in sight at the International School, where I sometimes do the school run. Places are almost impossible to get, so I try not to complain that my middle child is in a class of 24, despite fees of ¥1.8m (£10,136) a year. My eldest is at school in the UK in a class of 10, and enjoys extensive grounds and a nine-hole golf course, all for £12,000 a year.

The headmaster here is taking up a post as head of a UK prep school next year. I think he will find the parents more demanding than in Japan as, for the most part, they will be paying the fees out of their own pocket.

His legendary ability to charm expatriate mothers may not be quite so useful in Surrey.

One of the recent public holidays was Respect for the Aged Day. I am all for such events, especially as I get closer to 40 and my four-year-old asks me "Have you always been old, Mummy?"

The ageing population and falling birth rate are as much a concern in Japan as they are in every country that is committed to providing benefits to the elderly. To mark the recent public holiday, the government decided to give a gift to as many elderly people as it could. Several million cigarettes were distributed to all the old people's homes in Japan. One way to deal with the potential pension funding shortfall, I presume.

The Tokyo American Club provides a little home-from-home for the hundreds of US expatriates in the city. For those of us without a US passport, it is also a useful resource, since it possesses the best English-language library in the city and a 25-metre pool that doesn't require the wearing of bathing caps or a compulsory rest stop every half an hour, as Japanese pools do. However, the club costs ¥2m (£11,263) to join and has a monthly subscription of ¥26,000 (£146), and that's before you've bought a single beer.

The final straw for me, though, was being issued with a membership card boldly inscribed with a capital S, which clearly identifies me as someone's spouse. I don't wear a wedding ring for fear that a client will label me "domesticated mother" rather than "fearsome investment banker". Even if I were surreptitiously to slip my card to the waiter after entertaining a client, the game would be up when they returned the bill with my husband's name across the top.

A boutique coffee shop has just opened in the ground-floor of our building. I buy a coffee there every morning for ¥336 (£1.89), often at other times in the day, and also use it as an alternative meeting room. My annual coffee expenditure, therefore, comes to a..... small fortune. It would be cheaper to take up smoking and save our pension-fund trustees a few bob.

Mind you, it's always interesting to see what equity salesmen spend their money on. Our best salesman is a member of that rare breed, the Japanese career woman. She has no less than 10 Kelly Bags.

OCTOBER 23ᴿᴰ, 1999
THE ERECTION DEBATE
Nikkei 225: 17,438

My secretary passed out in the toilet last week. As she was taken away in an ambulance, my boss observed that this was not the first time that an employee of his had left the premises by this mode of transport. In this case, however, he denied any responsibility, especially when I suggested that she might be pregnant.

She returned to work after a few days looking as white as a sheet and no further questions have been asked. In a country where the low-dosage pill still does not have a licence after 10 years of clinical trials, unplanned pregnancies are common. Viagra, on the other hand, was fast-tracked to approval.

It is, therefore, not surprising that female university students in Japan are in favour of a mandatory retirement age for politicians. I discovered this while judging the finals of the English Speaking Union of Japan's annual debating competition last weekend.

This took place over a whole day and thoroughly tested my powers of concentration, not least because the Japanese do not have the sound "l" in their alphabet and tend to pronounce it "r", especially when engaged in a heated debate. As most of the topics were about politics, the word "election" cropped up regularly. The students were all in favour of more frequent and better-supported "elections". No wonder Viagra got its licence so quickly.

The yen has been living dangerously recently, skating around 100 to the dollar. While that makes the mental arithmetic easier when one is trying to work out exactly how much that ¥14,000 pedicure costs, it is going to make the chic little Honda sports car rather less competitive with the BMW Z3 in overseas markets. The movement in the currency has depressed the stock market and made lots of people here very agitated, none more so than my personal trainer, Bruce "The Body". His regular telephone calls and e-mails, ostensibly to check up on my daily eating and exercise routine, have been degenerating into discussions on hedging strategies. I would have thought that the ¥10,000 an hour I pay him was reward enough without needing free financial advice, but at least it's one way to get an attractive man to call me regularly.

While the Nikkei remains depressed, I have e-mailed my bank manager in London to instruct him to invest some more of my hard-won cash in a suitable Japanese fund. I have no time to select a suitable investment myself because any spare moments seem to be filled with reading pages and pages of information that come from the International School each week. No wonder they have had to move from individual reading to a "literacy hour" – most of the teacher's time must be spent writing newsletters.

I used to pass them straight to the nanny without opening them. However, a paragraph in the newsletter last week admonishing parents who hadn't sewn name tapes on items of uniform included the line: "Remember to tell 'the help'." Our Australian nanny has taken great offence at this description of her position and feels that it does not do justice to her NNEB qualification and experience. She obviously hasn't realised that having a father and brother who were first-class cricketers and another brother who played professional football were the real factors that counted on her CV when my (Australian) husband was reading it.

OCTOBER 30ᵀᴴ, 1999
GROWING PAINS
Nikkei 225: 17,924

The police have just raided the bank downstairs. This is about as exciting as the financial sector gets in Japan – 40 policemen inside the building, and 40 members of the press outside. I was glad it was a Thursday – we have dress-down Fridays here and I would have hated to be photographed in anything less than an Armani suit and a Hermes scarf.

Apparently, they cleared everyone's desk and took everything from the premises. The problem appears to be that the bank in question did not, at first, co-operate fully with the regulatory inspectors when they descended, unannounced, earlier in the year. The bank issued a statement saying it "did not understand" why it had been raided. I suspect it is a warning to all foreign-owned banks in Japan, my own included, that we had better co-operate with everyone from the minute they ring the doorbell.

Privately, I was delighted at this turn of events, as we have run out of office space and no other leases are likely to come up. I had thought about visiting some of the other tenants in the building and bidding for their space, but after the police visit I suspect our colleagues downstairs will be grateful for an opportunity to sublet.

We need more space, despite the fact that recruiting staff is as difficult as ever. I used to think that Russia represented the worst aspects of a free market out of control, but that was before I tried to hire people in what looks to be the start of an economic recovery in Japan. Retaining staff is also becoming a challenge; I get the impression that every executive search firm in Japan has suddenly gained access to our internal directory. My boss, who understands how to deal with Japanese staff, has explained to our human resources manager that any leak of information will result in my boss personally opening the window behind where the poor man sits, which is 17 stories up.

One of the few buildings in Tokyo taller than our office block is Tokyo Tower, a replica of the Eiffel Tower. Son Number Two was five last week, and has opted to take some of his friends on a visit there in lieu of a party. One mother, a very lovely Japanese lady, called to ask if there were any presents on the "banned" list. Thinking frantically about what she might buy, I assured her than any gift would be very generous and gratefully received. "Great," she said, "I'll pick up a hamster from the shop tomorrow".

Hamster or not, he is travelling to the UK this week to be pageboy at Staffordshire's wedding of the year. My Most Socially Acceptable Girlfriend is marrying a wonderful man that she met in a casino in Brisbane. Despite the lack of either a title or a grouse moor, her parents have supported the match and we're all looking forward to enjoying their hospitality (and using some of their 13 bathrooms). I haven't yet told my husband about the white tights and patent shoes that our son will be wearing for the occasion.

For a change, my husband and I will be travelling with our child. One of my personal horrors is the annual migration of the non-working expatriate wife. This phenomenon means that business class on the Japan-UK routes in early July and early September has children travelling on almost every flight. I prefer to send my children to the back of the plane with the nanny. Mind you, a seat at those times of the year is as difficult to get as a place at the International School, or a new bilingual employee. The free market is alive and well in Japan.

NOVEMBER 6TH, 1999
TOILET TRAINING
Nikkei 225: 18,354

"Mummy!" The shriek could be heard all over the house. We had gone to stay for the weekend with a Japanese colleague and his wife, a very pleasant and welcoming couple in their early 50s who have a weekend home on the south side of Mount Fuji. After I sprinted to see what was causing Son Number Two such alarm, I was met with a statement of shock and disbelief: "Mummy – the toilet seat is warm!" On reporting this back to my hostess, she expressed surprise that after the best part of 24 hours in their house, this was the first time my son had been to the loo. I had to remind her that, for boys, going to the loo and sitting on the seat were not necessarily one and the same activity.

Those of you familiar with Japanese five-star hotels will know that all the best establishments have heated toilet seats. In fact, they also have an array of controls in a panel beside the toilet that would not look out of place in the cockpit of a 747. I am usually too nervous to press any of the buttons, as they are all in Japanese and I worry that I might inadvertently give myself a colonic irrigation treatment.

One button that I did press while killing time in the toilet during a recent offsite management meeting was illustrated with some musical notes. When pressed, far from playing Beethoven's Fifth, it set off a pre-recorded audio track of a toilet being flushed. In Japan, ladies are embarrassed that others in the bathroom might hear the passing of wind or even matter of a more solid kind. Their preferred method of screening out the sound has been to continually flush the loo. When Tokyo's water table got to worryingly low levels, Toto, the largest manufacturer of toilets in Japan, launched a handy battery-operated gadget that makes a flushing noise when pressed. This nifty item can be easily carried in one's handbag and used as required, saving millions of gallons of water each year. In the prestigious hotel used for our meeting, they have thoughtfully added this function to the many on offer.

Bruce my trainer has made me promise to drink at least two litres of water a day and has bought me a 750cl water bottle for my desk that my secretary fills (and re-fills) from the cooler. This, of course, has increased my visits to the loo, much to my disgust. It's not so much the continued sounds of flushing that I can't bear, as the manic teeth-cleaning. All the Japanese girls in my office seem to clean their teeth four times daily. The bathroom is full of wash bags which they leave there, as they obviously haven't room in their (Kelly) handbags for these as well as the other necessary gadgets. I have tried to explain to Bruce the concept of the opportunity cost of time, but this appears to be beyond him. I shall have to instruct the office manager to buy some heated toilet seats, so at least my frequest visits to the loo will be comfortable.

NOVEMBER 13TH, 1999
WITHOUT A HITCH
Nikkei 225: 18.258

Getting married can be a very traumatic affair. I confess that I have only done it the once so far, and have no plans for a second attempt; my husband is still very much in situ and I would be hesitant to trade him in. After 11 years, I wouldn't know what to do with a man who'd prefer a candlelit dinner *à deux* to a TV dinner in front of the Golf Channel, and who races me to bed rather than staying up until 2am to watch the Rugby World Cup. My Single Girlfriend in Tokyo is hell bent on getting a marriage proposal out of someone in the next 12 months. I've suggested she find the one man on the planet who isn't interested in sport.

We were recently back in the UK for a wonderful wedding in Staffordshire. One of the Moneypenny offspring was a pageboy and behaved impeccably, despite having to wear a pair of tights for the first (and hopefully last) time in his life. After copious quantities of pink champagne at the reception, I staggered on to the evening function to find I had been seated next to a mildly well-known journalist who was fascinating on any topic provided it was Graham Greene. He did however know the name of the bride, which was more than could be said for the lady seated on the other side of him. She turned out to be the second wife of a friend of the bride's parents, which may account for her apparent amnesia.

While visiting the Midlands, the Moneypenny family stayed at a hostelry that is scheduled to host the next Ryder Cup in 2001. This had been booked and paid for in advance from Tokyo. Upon arrival, after 20 hours of travel, I was a little stunned to be given a room which I presume will be allocated to Tiger Woods's caddie's hairdresser's assistant in 2001. I had a word with the understanding manager the next day, and showed him a copy of this column. When he realised it was published on the same page as the hotel column, things looked up no end. Before my husband returned from his 18 holes of golf, we were all installed in the presidential suite.

In Japan the legal process of getting hitched involves filling out a form which you both sign, and then one of you can pop down to the ward office during your lunch hour to get it stamped. The ceremonial part, however, is big business. Tokyo has a bridal shop on almost every corner. Morning dress is as alive and well in Japan as it is in Staffordshire. The really fascinating thing is the number of "chapels" that have sprung up in all the smart hotels and even some restaurants. They usually have wooden pews, an altar, and a cross displayed in a prominent position. Some even have stained glass windows. Shinto ceremonies still take place but the number of "western-style" weddings, complete with the white dress, veil and the trumpet voluntary outstrips any other kind by a large multiple. The huge demand for such occasions has caused a severe shortage in the availability of clergy, choirs and trumpet players. An ad for such in the paper recently said: "ordained clergy required to conduct wedding ceremonies; churchgoers considered".

The honeymoon is also a big event. The high price of property in Japan virtually ensures that people do not cohabit before marriage, and sometimes have to continue to live with one family or the other after becoming man and wife. The honeymoon is therefore the first time that many couples will have spent so much time in one another's company. I am reliably informed that a recent phenomenon is the "Narita divorce". Narita is the name of Tokyo's international airport and a "Narita divorce" refers to the practice whereby the whole white wedding takes place, followed by the honeymoon, prior to visiting the ward office. If the couple feel that, after two weeks on honeymoon, they don't fancy a lifetime together, the paper is never filed. I should, of course, have tried this myself and scheduled my honeymoon during a Test Match. I have a feeling Mr Moneypenny might still be single.

NOVEMBER 20TH, 1999
DID THE EARTH MOVE FOR YOU?
Nikkei 225: 18,570

Last Monday evening was a disaster. It was deliberately so. The Women's Group at the Tokyo American Club held its annual disaster-awareness evening. This involves, among other things, being shown in graphic detail what devastation an earthquake can wreak on a large city, such as Tokyo, using photographs of the 1995 Kobe disaster. It also offers practical advice on the ways in which citizens should prepare themselves for such an event, including the requisite rations to be held in readiness in the larder. The fire service kindly provides the opportunity to practice crawling through a smoke-filled room, navigating by feeling along the walls. Most dignified.

Last year, I was out of town for the occasion and urged my husband to attend so that we could be well prepared for the next big earthquake in Tokyo. Sadly, he was otherwise engaged and I have had to rely on other mothers at the International School who have attended over the years. One thing they made clear to me is that my plan to send the nanny this year was perhaps misplaced if I was hoping she would stay much longer with us in Japan – apparently, the exercise is truly frightening. As I panic at the smallest thing going bump in the night, and can't face any film with the slightest hint of violence, I think the disaster-awareness evening will have to suffer the same fate as *Reservoir Dogs*, and manage without a viewing by myself. I shall read the *Minato Ward Disaster Handbook* instead. Reading the book instead of seeing the film was exactly how I managed to share appreciation of *The Silence of the Lambs*.

Actually, there are about 1,000 earthquakes a year in Japan, most of which can only be detected by specialist seismic-monitoring equipment. Most of them occur in the Kanto region, in which Tokyo is situated. Tokyo itself has not had a big earthquake since 1923, when it was struck by one that destroyed about a third of the city. On average, Tokyo has had a major earthquake every 60 years or so, so the city is well overdue for one now.

It might not have registered on any seismic monitoring equipment, but there was a Big Bang in Japan on October 1. Not an earthquake, but a big bang such as took place in the UK in 1986 – the deregulation of stock market commissions. Stockbrokers in Japan, finally, have had to face what most of the world has had to for years – that clients can, and will, use their strength to pay minimal commissions. As in 1986 (or indeed 1923), not everyone will survive. I am hoping this will provide rich pickings in my long-running search for employees.

We remain on standby for an earthquake, and the nanny tells me that almost all the mothers at the International School have stocked up against the day the supermarket is destroyed. I confess to having done nothing, apart from ensure that we have the requisite water supplies (three litres per person per day) and some spare batteries for the torch. Looking in the larder, I can see that if we survive, we will be living on baby-milk formula, salsa and tinned spaghetti. Oh, and tomato ketchup.

We have had several earthquakes in the year I've lived in Tokyo, but somehow I have missed them all, or maybe it's not that easy to tell.

My Single Girlfriend tells me that her first earthquake experience was at 3am. She awoke, her then boyfriend beside her, to find the bed shaking. She turned over and addressed her then boyfriend in the dark. "Hugh!" she said. "What *are* you doing?"

NOVEMBER 27ᵀᴴ, 1999
THE REEL THING
Nikkei 225: 18,914

"Call yourself a banker – you can't even draw the figure eight!" This observation on my numeracy was given, unsolicited, not by my boss but by the girl dancing next to me at last week's final rehearsal for the St Andrew's Day Ball. Fortunately, just after this comment had been passed, a senior executive at a rival bank, (indeed, a bank which boasts Scots origins), chose to go the wrong way round in the "ring of hands" section of the eightsome reel. Reeling is a great leveller.

Tokyo may be full of Japanese, but it has its fair share of Scots, too. These come in varying degrees of authenticity, from the lovely man who runs the St Andrew's Society (whose accent sounds as though he has never been south of the border), to several hundred Japanese people who feel a strong affinity with the country that invented both whisky and golf.

Drinking whisky and playing golf are both pursuits followed by the vast majority of Japanese men. There is even an annual Highland Games. I have to say there is something disconcerting about seeing large numbers of Japanese people sporting Highland dress and performing impressive displays of both dancing and music in suburban Tokyo on a Saturday afternoon. However, the Japanese frame is, on the whole, slighter than that of the average Scot. So both this year and last, no entrant has succeeded in tossing the caber, and the spectators have had to make do with a demonstration from the judge who had flown in for the event.

The Japanese fondness for haggis is starting to make more sense to me now that I have lived here for a while. One of my favourite Japanese foods prior to moving here was *yakatori*, which in Japanese restaurants in the UK and elsewhere is presented as chunks of chicken breast on a skewer which has been grilled over charcoal. In Japan, there is no shortage of restaurants dedicated to this type of cuisine and I couldn't wait to start sampling them.

Chicken yakatori was the first thing I ordered. Sure enough, the chicken breast slices on a skewer appeared. Then, one after another, almost every other part of the chicken did, too. As we worked our way through the organs of the chicken, I have to confess to feeling more squeamish with each course. I should counter this by saying I unreservedly love Japanese food, and it is always my number one choice to eat at a Japanese restaurant. But in the same way that Chinese restaurants in London SW3 bear little resemblance to those in China, Japanese restaurants in Japan are an entirely different eating experience. A restaurant has just opened round the corner from us which is entirely devoted to the eating of eel.

I own one long dress suitable for Scottish dancing, but failed to locate it after a long search. I therefore decided to make a long skirt and after purchasing the material last weekend, dug out the sewing machine. I then realised that the machine (along with every other electrical household good we own) did not like Japan's 110-volt current. When I finally found the transformer (attached to Mr M's trouser press), it decided to pack up. Finally defeated, I did the whole thing by hand. When I tried on the finished article, I thought it prudent to check that it went well with my evening jacket. As I removed the jacket from the hanger, there underneath it was the *original* long dress.

My battle to exercise more continues. I resorted to wearing my heart-rate monitor to the ball rehearsal and was gratified to see that I had expended a total of 867 calories during the one hour and 45 minutes that I spent galloping around.

The monitor stores all exercise data and I proudly showed it to Bruce the trainer the next day. He was somewhat intrigued as to what specific activity had been responsible for the workout, and even went as far as to ask if Mr M had shared in it with me. I was pleased to reply in the affirmative. Mr M needs as much reeling practice as me.

DECEMBER 4ᵀᴴ, 1999
SLEEP TIGHT
Nikkei 225: 18,368

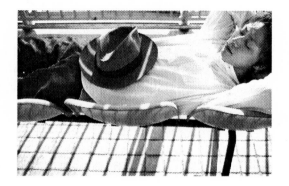

The telephone rang at 2.30am. I awoke from a deep sleep, my heart racing, convinced that something terrible had happened. At the other end a 10-year-old boy greeted me warmly, assured me that there was nothing wrong and that he just wanted to know if he could go ice-skating in Basingstoke that weekend.

Managing children at a distance can be a challenge, and I am the first to admit it. My husband pointed out the other day that, at that precise moment, we had children on three continents: the eldest at prep school in the UK, the middle one at home in Japan with us, and the baby with his nanny visiting her parents in Australia for two weeks. While this last arrangement might seem unusual, the nanny (and her parents) have been well known to us for years. My only cause for concern was when I found my husband giving instructions regarding the baby's care in Australia. Rather than the usual lecture about sunscreen and a hat, he was encouraging the nanny to let her father, a former first-class cricketer, hold the baby as often as possible. I presume he thinks sporting talent can be passed on by osmosis.

Here in Japan, telephone calls notwithstanding, I am trying to get all the sleep I can. I have worked out that if I allocate the appropriate time to each task I am supposed to undertake each day, I need 17 hours. which leaves seven hours a day for sleep, meals, having a shower and going to the loo. The Japanese are a great example of how to make the most of

33

every day. They seem to have perfected the art of catnapping anywhere, anytime. The lengthy commutes that most Japanese working in Tokyo are forced to endure should, in theory, provide an excellent opportunity to catch up on lost sleep. However, there are precious few seats and almost everyone has to stand. Last week I was shown the latest invention – it resembles a tall music stand with a headrest, allowing one to rest one's head while standing on the train. The height is adjustable, so presumably the manufacturers are hoping to develop an export market.

Whether they commute or not, most Japanese carry handkerchiefs. These are not used to blow one's nose – blowing noses in public, and particularly in restaurants, is the height of rudeness in Japan. No, the handkerchiefs are used to dab their brows to mop up excessive perspiration. The packed trains and constant climbing up and down stairs and escalators at stations mean most *sararimen* arrive at work covered in sweat, whatever the time of year.

Mind you, it's not just the Japanese. The beautiful wife of a rival bank manager in Tokyo was also using a (designer) handkerchief for perspiration control last weekend, at the St Andrew's Ball. I must confess that somewhere between *Strip the Willow* and *The Duke of Perth*, I wished that I had put one in Mr M's sporran before we left home. I am afraid I was forced to use one of the Tokyo Hilton's napkins.

As well as staying up to dance reels, I have been getting up even earlier than usual, for a spate of breakfast meetings. I have mixed views on these, as I find it hard to talk, take notes and eat simultaneously, let along converse quietly enough so that the people on the next table are not privy to the bank's entire business strategy for the next year. However, I willingly went to a breakfast meeting last Friday with the utterly charming Lord Currie of Marylebone. He was in Tokyo to drum up support for the London Business School, of which I am an alumnus. But my plans to ask his views on the Bank of Japan's zero interest rate policy went adrift when I suddenly notice what amazing brown eyes he has. Only 22 per cent of students on the MBA programme at the LBS are female. If they want to increase this, I suggest they send Lord Currie out on the road more often.

The Moneypenny family will be on the road itself soon. We have decided to convene on one continent, *terra australis*, for the Christmas holidays and the start of 2000. This should, temporarily at least, mean that I get some uninterrupted sleep.

DECEMBER 11ᵀᴴ, 1999
HEADS DOWN
Nikkei 225: 18,271

The lights all went out at 10.30am the other day. I was standing on the dealing floor, talking to my boss, when they flickered and then failed. In the few seconds it took for the back-up generator to spring into action, my corporate life flashed before my eyes; what exactly was the contingency plan? Had the computer line to the Tokyo Stock Exchange gone down? Were we in the middle of a trade? Was it an earthquake? I still hadn't ordered that fireproof filing cabinet.

Fortunately, we are in an office block well prepared for such eventualities, and we were only without power for 10 seconds. The other 799,999 properties that receive power from the same source as us were not so lucky. The electricity-generating company was prepared for an earthquake, but not for a Japanese military jet to crash into its main power lines. Some households were without power for more than 24 hours. There was the statutory press conference at which the managers bowed deeply to express their apologies for the incident.

Bowing technique is very important in Japan, and I still haven't quite grasped its finer points. For day-to-day greetings of one's peers, a brief inclination of the head and the top of the shoulders seems acceptable. When saying "thank you", the shoulders have to go down further. For greeting senior people, a much deeper bow is necessary. An apology is a 90-degree job, and a mega-apology requires kneeling down and bowing one's forehead to the floor.

I helped to host a lunch earlier this year for Ian Macfarlane, the governor

35

of the Reserve Bank of Australia, at which several senior Japanese clients were present. Having spent 20 minutes bowing, I carried on, even when introduced to Mr Macfarlane. My boss, who was behind me, reminded me my legs don't bear any resemblance to Elle Macpherson's and perhaps I should wear longer skirts.

I was in Hong Kong on business this week. While I was there, I did visit my dressmaker and asked her to lengthen all my skirts by several inches. The differences between Hong Kong and Tokyo are many, not least that buildings in Tokyo do not have a "ground floor". I kept getting into lifts to find myself one floor above my intended destination.

I used to live in Hong Kong, but managed to get The Bank to post me elsewhere before the handover to the Chinese. I wasn't worried about any potential loss of political freedom, but I knew that life would never be the same after the British military presence pulled out and closed down its radio station. The British Forces Broadcasting Service has the highly sensible policy (not adopted by the World Service, I am sad to say) of including the omnibus edition of *The Archers* in its weekly programming.

When I moved to Singapore, and later to Tokyo, I was saved from *Archers* deprivation by a man I have never met, but who has become one of the most important in my life. His name is Chris Harrison, and he is not only a doctoral student at Imperial College London, but also the vice-captain of Vesta Rowing Club.

I can't imagine his thesis is progressing very quickly as he maintains a website where every day a summary of the latest *Archers* episode is posted (www.lowfield.co.uk/archers/). The site also cross-references to plot summaries and press cuttings – most useful for those of us who've forgotten whom Cathy had an affair with. The BBC did eventually realise that this was a good idea and you can now get the same information at www.bbc.co.uk/radio4/archers. This week an apology appears on Chris' site – Vesta's annual dinner was scheduled for Friday, so Friday's plot summary might be a bit late.

One of the most stressful meetings that I had in Hong Kong was not at the office, but with my supervisor at Hong Kong University's School of Business. I, too, am a doctoral student. I enrolled in 1995, and my progress has been about as fast as Mr Harrison's. I don't have the excuse of having to keep the wired world up-to-date on *The Archers*, but I do have a full-time job and three children. Oh, and a fireproof filing cabinet to order.

DECEMBER 18TH, 1999
GIFT RAP
Nikkei 225: 18,095

The Christmas tree outside the office building went up in early November. The one in the coffee shop downstairs appeared even earlier, and they switched to using seasonally decorated red cups, instead of the usual white. It finally dawned on me that Christmas in Japan was on the way when I went to buy some udon noodles and sauce from the Japanese supermarket across the street from the office, and had my hearing assaulted by the sounds of Slade's "Merry Christmas" played over the PA system. I wonder if Noddy Holder knows that Japanese housewives are selecting their shitake mushrooms to his dulcet tones.

I had fled back to the UK to give birth to my youngest last year, so I missed all this. I was going to brave a Japanese maternity ward, until I realised that my Japanese wasn't going to be good enough to say "Get me an anaesthetist *now*." As I need an anaesthetic to have my legs waxed, access to pain relief is a high priority in any Moneypenny birth plan.

As Christmas approaches, gift-giving is starting to preoccupy my thoughts. This is not just because the antipodean branch of the Moneypenny family, with whom we shall be staying, now numbers 18 people. It is actually the Japanese gift-giving protocol that I am struggling to get my head around. Last week, I presented one of my hardest-working employees with a set of baby clothes for the newest addition to his family. This week a package appeared on my desk, beautifully wrapped, containing two exquisite sake cups, together with a note from the baby's mother, thanking me for my gift.

Upon enquiry, I discovered that good Japanese manners require gift recipients to (a) assess how much the giver has spent and (b) purchase a return gift of approximately half the value by way of thanks. As I had bought the baby clothes in Marks and Spencer, which has not yet opened in Japan, I don't know how they estimated the money I had spent. Judging by the sake cups, they were presuming me to be rather more generous than I was! I also wasn't sure if this orgy of reciprocal gift-giving should continue – was I supposed to give them one sake cup in return?

Weddings and funerals in Japan are occasions for giving money, but there is another round of etiquette surrounding this as well. Sums of money starting with a four are definitely out, especially for a wedding, as four can also signify death. For weddings, odd-numbered multiples of ¥1,000 are appropriate, since an even number can be divided by two, which might indicate that you expect the recipient to get married a second time. The hosts of these occasions are then expected to open all the envelopes, buy all the givers a gift to half the value of the money received, and write them a thank-you note.

The Japanese also give "summer" and "winter" gifts, usually from one company to another to thank them for their business over the past six months. My experience of this is from Mr M, who is sent sets of tablecloths, bottles of whisky and boxes of peculiar-looking sweets by various advertising agencies. Fortunately, compliance rules in Japan have almost eliminated this practice between banks and their clients, otherwise I can see it becoming incredibly expensive, quite apart from the challenge of thinking up things to give every six months.

No problem with thinking up a present for the nanny this year – I am going to try and give her a boyfriend. To this end, I recently arranged a blind date with the latest recruit to our office. I'm not sure how the date went; I suspect he may have what the locals call "yellow fever" – a disease common among many expatriate men in Asia, where people have a predilection for Asian, rather than Caucasian, sexual partners. I will monitor the situation closely. He did send round some flowers and a bottle of Dom Pérignon afterwards. He may not get the appropriate gift in return. I haven't yet seen a half-bottle of DP in Japan. Happy Christmas!

JANUARY 8TH, 2000
IN THE BLACK
Nikkei 225: 18,193

Japan will never have a millennium. At least, not until the life expectancy of the imperial family lengthens quite considerably. At midnight on December 31, the year ceased to be Heisei 11 (the 11th year of the "clarity and "harmony" era) and started to be Heisei 12. The year is dated according to the length of the emperor's reign. Despite the fact that the emperor of Japan was revered as a god until after the Second World War, none of them has ever lived for 1,000 years.

The last emperor, Hirohito, died in the year that you and I know as 1989. To the Japanese, it was Showa ("shining peace") 64. It was also one of the shortest years on record in Japan because it only lasted a week – he died on January 7th. January 8th 1989 was therefore the first day of Heisei 1. This must have played havoc with all the dating required for official documents, train tickets, in fact anything at all that emanates from a government source.

I wish Emperor Akhito the best of health and happiness and a long reign, but if he is ever planning to abdicate, then a good date to suggest would be December 31st, and preferably with 12 months' advance warning.

Some 30 people were on compulsory millennium duty in my office in Japan. I'm afraid that my only contribution was to approve the sushi order for them, just before leaving for Sydney. I broke the habit of a lifetime and travelled in economy with my children, just to remind myself what it was like.

The answer is cramped, hot and uncomfortable, plus very noisy from all the other children around. The 747 allocated by the airline for the Tokyo-Sydney route that day had a spiral staircase, which, as every frequent traveller knows, is indicative of the advanced age of the plane. The lack of in-seat entertainment in economy also had two unpleasant side effects: a bored five-year-old, and a one-year-old whose cot was immediately below the film screen. Fortunately, the nanny was prepared for this; before she departed to use my seat in business class, she produced appropriate drugs to ensure that the one-year-old did not wake up at all during the flight.

Her other great achievement was to locate a supply of HP Sauce within hours of arrival in Sydney. This means that the usual complaints from my 10-year-old about how boarding school food is infinitely better than anything at home will be somewhat muted. It is definitely time to renew her contract. My husband agrees with me, but I suspect his favourable view is unrelated to the HP sauce. The nanny's eldest brother was appointed chief executive of a leading football club in Melbourne just before Christmas.

Of course, I may not be able to afford her. The boom year in Japan in 1999 means that many investment bankers have already been, or are about to be, paid record bonuses. One of the nannies known to us in Tokyo works for a family where the father is employed by a famous US bulge-bracket firm. Just before Christmas, he was notified of his bonus for 1999. Quite rightly, he chose to give a very generous Christmas bonus to the nanny. This has unfortunately set the standard in Tokyo.

Bonuses dominate the first part of any calendar year for me and anyone else involved in the management of investment banking. The year 2000, or Heisei 12, will be no exception. My evenings and weekends will be spent poring over spreadsheets, attempting to remember which Suzuki is which. The Japanese have very few surnames. The name Suzuki is the most common, accounting for some 20 per cent of the population. People in Japan are always called by their surnames, so Suzuki-san the driver is addressed, and referred to, in the same way as Suzuki-san the derivatives salesman. The suffix "san" is the Japanese way of saying "Mr/Mrs/Miss", except it never changes, either with sex or marital status.

If I am not careful, massive over- (or under-) compensation could occur. Fortunately, out of the 100,000-plus people working for my bank worldwide, I am the only Moneypenny, so let's hope that the correct bonus finds its way to my account.

JANUARY 15TH, 2000
HOME TRUTHS
Nikkei 225: 18,956

Flying for 22 hours from London to Sydney was not enough. A week after his arrival, citing his better-than-usual school report, Son Number One begged me to let him visit his friend in Adelaide as a reward. I groaned, not just because of the expense, but because I know that when I rang the airline, I would have to give them my credit card billing address in Japan.

Explaining a Japanese address to someone not based in Japan is always stressful. Addresses in Japan are full of hyphens and numbers, as well as unfamiliar-sounding districts. They also don't help you to find the house or flat they describe.

Japanese addresses identify the district in which one lives by name, but this merely narrows the area down to several square kilometres. The three digits attached to the name give greater clues. The first of these identifies the "chome" or subdistrict, and is usually the extent of any taxi driver's knowledge, being a mere two square kilometres or so.

The second digit tells you which part of the subdistrict the property is in, which means you are down to about half a square kilometre. The final part is the hardest – the third digit. This refers to the plot of land on which the property is built, and these are numbered in the order in which they were built. Therefore, plot 25 will be nowhere near plot 24, and may have several houses located on it. Our address is shared by no fewer than five other houses.

Of course, this anachronism of Japanese life means that telephoning for a pizza or inviting people round for dinner becomes a huge challenge. In Tokyo, more than anywhere in the world, people rely on both the fax machine and the work of thousands of amateur cartographers. If you order a pizza from a place you haven't used before, you will have to fax a map of how to find you.

Maps are to be found on the back of business cards, and in advertisements for shops – in fact, everywhere, usually in both Japanese and English. It is unusual to find an expatriate who doesn't have a home *meishi* (business card), complete with a map on the back of how to find them. No wonder the Japanese install global positioning systems in their cars as a matter of course.

While my son navigated his way to Adelaide, Mr M took me away for a couple of days to the Blue Mountains, ostensibly to celebrate a wedding anniversary. We stayed in an establishment that Mr M had selected, I suspect, mainly for its access to satellite television. We spent our time either in the room watching the Australia-India test match on TV or driving around listening to it on the radio. After dinner each evening, we retired to the room to... watch the England-South Africa test match.

While down in Sydney for the Christmas break, I managed to exercise almost every day. Most days this consisted of puffing and panting round a football ground near the house we were renting. One morning, I persuaded my son to accompany me on a bicycle for moral support. I instructed him to cycle beside me and issue encouraging words. Five minutes into the session came the first of these. "Mum," he said, "you're looking thinner already". I knew he deserved that trip to Adelaide.

JANUARY 22ND, 2000
GOOD HAIR DAY
Nikkei 225: 18,878

Left, right and straight on. These are the three most important expressions to learn to say in Japanese before spending any length of time in Tokyo. They will enable you to direct a taxi driver to where you want to go, assuming that you know the way. Similarly, the most essential publication to own is the Bilingual Metropolitan Road Atlas, a sort of A-Z but without a street index. The reason for this, as I described before, is that more than 95 per cent of the streets in Tokyo have no name. Key buildings are the important things to learn, navigating by landmarks being standard practice. I live around the corner from the worldwide headquarters of a famous Japanese car company and work next door to the best-known hotel in the city, so that makes life easy.

I reflected on this when I opened my laptop computer to write this piece and stared in puzzlement at the short pieces of hair scattered across the keyboard. I suddenly recalled that I had last used it three days previously while having my hair done. My personal frustration with hairdressers is their complete lack of understanding about the opportunity cost of my time. However, personal vanity dictates that regular visits are necessary, and from time to time I have to grit my teeth and spend more than two hours there while somebody lovingly wraps bits of my hair in silver foil to make it lighter than it would be otherwise. The ongoing nightmare of bonus season means that two hours are two more than I can afford to spend out of the office.

My new computer only has one-and-a-half hours of battery time, so I set off for the hairdresser glumly, expecting to have to spend half an hour looking at magazines full of women thinner than me. I had forgotten how well supplied with power points a hairdressing salon is – I sat in three different seats during the appointment and all were handily supplied with power, of course designed to accommodate hairdryers rather than the laptop computers of stressed investment bankers. This experience has transformed my view of visits to the hairdresser. Two hours of dedicated work time, with no telephone interruptions and a convenient power supply – what more could a girl ask for?

Driving to the hairdresser along Tokyo's narrow streets reminded me of my first days of driving in this city. When I approached my first "narrow passing opportunity", I stopped, got out of the car, folded in each wing mirror and manoeuvred my way past. After doing this for the third time in one short journey, I felt completely exhausted. It was only later that some kind soul showed me the button that all cars in Japan come with, which automatically folds both wing mirrors against the car for easier passage through narrow places. What a fool I must have looked.

No worse, though, than the friend of mine who drives a splendid American 4WD around town and used to get lost, often late at night after visiting some unknown district. On more than one occasion, he had to stop his car, hail a passing taxi, and pay it to lead him back home. Now that he knows the way, he has learned the three magic words and catches the cab himself. In case you ever visit they are *migi, hidari* and *massugu.*

JANUARY 29TH, 2000
FLOOR SHOW
Nikkei 225: 19,434

We all need new socks. One of the most important items of clothing in Japan, socks take on a whole new significance when living and working in Tokyo. Entering someone's house, a smart restaurant, a shrine, the gym or even a hotel room requires one to shed shoes and pad about either in your socks, or slippers that are supplied by the establishment. Then, when you go to the toilet, you change out of these into "toilet slippers", another pair that are usually a different colour so you don't confuse them.

The Japanese would hate to think that footwear which had been in contact with the toilet floor might touch the floor in the rest of the house, even though, thanks to the Japanese obsession with cleanliness, you could eat off any toilet floor in the country. Far worse than wearing toilet slippers outside their natural home would be to tread on *tatami* flooring in outdoor shoes or even bare feet. Tatami is the straw-like weed that is used to manufacture traditional Japanese floor-coverings. These days, it's used mostly in bedrooms, but in many of the tiny homes in Tokyo, it covers the floor of the principal room which by day serves as the living room. At night, the futons are brought out and laid on the tatami.

Futons in Japan are nothing like the ones that you buy in the UK; they are more like thick duvets or thin, foam mattresses. The tatami provides an additional springy layer.

My familiarity with tatami has increased as my negotiations to rent extra office space have reached their nadir. We are finally due to sign a lease tomorrow to give us half of another floor in the building. The continuing suggestions of economic recovery in Japan have led almost every part of our bank – and many others – to want to set up shop here, so space is in short supply. I won't believe we really have the space until I see the company stamp on the lease, but neither my staff nor the landlord will sign until tomorrow, as it is an auspicious day in the Buddhist calendar. Sometimes I can hardly believe that Japan is in the G7.

The new space is not covered with tatami, and we are not proposing to install it, but I had to learn very quickly how many tatami mats would fit into it. This is because the principal unit of area in Japan is the *tsubo*. One tsubo equals two tatami mats. Are you any the wiser?

I finally managed to get someone to explain to me that a tatami mat measures 1.8m by 0.9m. This is not a joke – commercial rents in Japan are quoted in yen per tsubo per month. When I did my MBA, they never told me that one of my toughest management tasks would be to estimate how many tatami mats made up one dealing-desk.

It is not only in Japanese homes that I pad around in socks; I also like to go shoeless in aeroplanes. Arriving in first class last week, I noticed that the cabin service director was lurking in the galley rather than greeting passengers. One of the other stewards came forward and asked me if I was, indeed, Mrs Moneypenny. When I replied in the affirmative, the director finally emerged and breathed a sigh of relief. It turned out that one of his (three) ex-wives had exactly the same name as me and, having seen it on the manifest, he had decided to hide until he knew that I wasn't her.

I shall be back on an aeroplane again next week, returning to the UK to reassure my superiors that all is well in the land of the rising sun. With the Nikkei still north of 18,000 and continuing to rise, I do not anticipate any problems. Of course, it still has a way to go. As we entered the past decade, it had peaked at over 38,000. My first call next week will be to Marks and Spencer – to buy some more socks.

FEBRUARY 5TH, 2000
SLIPPERY SLOPES
Nikkei 225: 19,763

Gordon Brown had packed his overcoat. That was just as well, because the weekend he visited Tokyo for the G7 finance ministers' meeting, it was cold.

I cycled to the gym on the morning of the meeting, dodging roadworks as I went. For decades, the construction industry has been the Japanese government's preferred channel for pumping money into the economy, which is presumably completely unrelated to the fact that it is also one of the most generous fillers of the ruling party's coffers. Tokyo at night becomes a different place, with roadworks springing up in even larger numbers, specifically over the sites of the new underground line.

My personal trainer, Bruce the gorgeous Canadian, would have been delighted to see me in the gym that Saturday morning. He apparently called up just before 9am, only to be told by my housekeeper that I was still asleep in bed. I felt so guilty about this that I leapt into my gym kit and grabbed my bike. Still, I did manage to meet him at the gym at 7am one day last week, which I consider nothing less than Herculean for a woman with three children and a full-time job.

Poor Bruce does not seem to appreciate the cold, despite coming from an unpronounceable town in British Columbia where it snows constantly. I suspect it is because his thinning hair requires him to wear a handkerchief over his head to cut heat loss, making him look like an extra from *The Pirates of Penzance*.

This is, of course, the perfect weather for skiing. Japan is a skier's and snowboarder's heaven, full of resorts enjoying plenty of snow. The investment in infrastructure means that you can catch the bullet train to the slopes from Tokyo in an hour.

I am still struggling with the office redesign, and have taken to going to the toilet on another floor in the building. This is so I cannot be ambushed, as has started to happen frequently, by women who want to explain exactly why their particular desk cannot be moved. Many years ago, when I first joined the bank, my then boss warned me that, of all management tasks, reorganising seating arrangements was simply the worst, eclipsing even wholesale sackings.

That boss is still with the bank, but has long since been promoted to the stratosphere, so I rarely get to see him. He did, however, visit Japan last week, and made the mistake of trying to engage our most senior Japanese saleswoman in small talk. He asked her if she skied in Japan. No one had explained to him that this was as appropriate as asking her whether her Kelly handbag was a fake, or if she bought her suits at M&S. Now that skiing is accessible to so much of the Japanese population, the only way to differentiate oneself socially and avoid incredibly crowded slopes is to nip over the Pacific to the Rocky Mountains.

I took the junior foreigners in the office out for dinner recently, and was interested to learn that they considered Alan Greenspan the most influential man in the world's financial markets. I asked the three of them – all boys, average age 24 – how old Mr Greenspan was, given that he has just been appointed for a further four-year term at the Fed. Guesses ranged from 62 to 70. Mr Greenspan is, however, 73, the same age as my father-in-law, and the age my own father will turn in 2001.

Both are retired, but if they feel that 73 is time to work for another four years, I shall suggest that they come to Japan and become construction site "policemen", waving on traffic and keeping pedestrians out of danger. This is compulsory for all building sites and provides employment for several hundred people of Mr Greenspan's age. Maybe construction really is boosting the economy.

FEBRUARY 12TH, 2000
FAT CITY
Nikkei 225: 19,710

I spent a couple of nights with Mike Tyson the other week. Well, we slept under the same roof, at any rate. On a brief visit to the UK, I found I was booked into the same hostelry as the boxer's entourage, which made getting in and out of the building past the hordes of journalists a challenge.

Sumo wrestlers in Japan have the same celebrity status as Mr Tyson, but never need anything so undignified as a police escort to get them from a hotel to a car. Sumo involves many quasi-religious rituals – legend has it that the Japanese race was founded after a sumo bout when a god beat the leader of a rival tribe. Even allowing for myth, sumo is more than 1,500 years old; originally, it was a religious ritual performed in prayer for a successful harvest. There are only six grand tournaments a year in Japan, three in Tokyo. You get more value for money as a spectator than you did watching Mr Tyson the other weekend; the tournament (called, appropriately, a *basho*) lasts 15 days with multiple bouts each day.

A ticket buys you a seat for one day only. Those nearest the action are the most pricey, and the most dangerous, since a bout is won by either forcing the opponent on to the ground or throwing him out of the ring.

Although sumo matches outside Japan are rare, the Japanese do venture overseas. Two preferred activities when flying are smoking, which is almost completely banned these days on the world's airlines, and undoing their seatbelts, standing up and getting down their luggage, the minute the aircraft's wheels touch the ground.

The cabin service director on my flight to the UK had the measure of his passengers. After a warning about disabling smoke alarms, he announced that "anyone found smoking will be put out on the wing, where, if they can light up, they can smoke".

A silence followed, not because the passengers were shocked, but because the Japanese crew member beside him refused to translate his words. Undeterred, he tried again as we touched down at Heathrow: "Ladies and gentlemen, welcome to London. We have just received a message from the control tower asking us to clean the toilets before disembarking. If anyone wishes to assist, will they please stand up."

A benefit of being in the UK was the chance to see the eldest Moneypenny offspring, who is incarcerated in an English prep school. Mr M selected this establishment for him on the grounds that (a) Douglas Jardine had gone there, and (b) that year the school had old boys captaining the cricket first XI in three top public schools.

The poor child will probably struggle to make even the under-11 B-team this summer, but I am relieved to report that some academic progress is being made. He has developed a keen interest in geography, which I suspect has more to do with the headmaster taking that class than the fact that I have hauled him around the world since he was four years old.

The school provides (and launders) all sports uniforms throughout the time the boy is there – for a one-off fee at the start. This represents great value for money, especially when you see the wear-and-tear they get. The outfits worn by Messrs Tyson and Julius in Manchester will presumably be worn only once.

Sumo contestants are naked except for a heavy silk loincloth. This garment is about 10 yards long and two feet wide; it is folded in six along its length and then wrapped around the waist several times, the exact number being determined by the girth of the contestant.

The longest part of a sumo bout is the *shikiri*, when the two contestants intersperse glaring at each other with the occasional throwing of handfuls of salt on the ground to purify the ring and protect them from injuries. This goes on for up to four minutes before they actually engage, after which time one wrestler usually disposes of the other one very quickly. Just like Mr Tyson, in fact.

FEBRUARY 19ᵀᴴ, 2000
TRY THAT FOR SIZE
Nikkei 225: 19,789

How long are your feet in centimetres? You might care to measure them, especially if you are planning a business trip to Japan and want to use a gym. You can walk in off the street, as everything is for hire, but the Japanese shoe size system might floor you unless you have a tape measure to hand.

I am attending the gym regularly but, sadly, could still earn a living as a double for Dawn French. I would sack my personal trainer, but he is too cute. Anyway, I suspect my partiality for ordering mocha with whipped cream may be the cause. I have often fancied a career as an actress, but doubt whether anyone would cast me in a nude scene, particularly after three caesarean sections. Sex scenes on the radio might be OK, such as the recent shower scene in *The Archers*. I didn't hear this episode myself, despite the kind FT reader who wrote to tell me that the BBC now broadcasts Radio 4 on the web, because I am so technologically illiterate that I have yet to successfully download Real Playex.

I understand that reference was made to Jolene "slipping out of her kimono". I doubt very much that Jolene has a kimono – very few women wear them in Tokyo, let alone in deepest Borsetshire. A kimono is the traditional dress of a Japanese woman, usually made of heavy silk

53

and secured by an *obi*, an ornately embroidered piece of material that goes several times around the waist before being folded and secured elaborately at the back. Getting into or out of one of these garments takes quite a while.

I suspect Jolene was actually wearing a *yukata*, a cotton dressing gown that people of either sex get changed into after getting home from the office or after a bath. Yukata are provided by Japanese hotels for guests, and it is not uncommon to see people wearing them in the dining room. I get into a complete panic when presented with one as I can never remember whether it is supposed to be worn with the right side crossing the left or vice versa. The distinction is important – one way is used for dressing corpses. After staying up until 2am several nights this week trying to sort out the 1999 bonuses, I feel a bit like the living dead, so maybe it doesn't matter which way I wear my yukata.

Working late enabled me to meet the nanny and Son Number Two on their return from Hokkaido, the large island in the north of Japan, when they got in late the other night. After the baby had been allowed to go on holiday with the nanny last October, it was only fair that the others should get a turn. She took Son Number Two to the annual snow festival in Sapporo, where the most fantastic ice sculptures are built, usually incorporating a slide or something interactive, making the whole place like a frozen theme park. He loved every minute. I doubt that Son Number One will go away with the nanny, whatever the destination. He would be too worried that she would divert at the last moment to a health farm. He finds her insistence on vegetables at almost every meal to be far too rigorous a dietary regime.

The nanny does sometimes manage to go away with her friends, unencumbered by children. Visiting a town in the south of Japan, she stayed at an inn and put on the yukata provided. It was in the evening, and, as is the custom, people were walking to and from the public baths in yukata. The correct footwear for such public promenading is a pair of wooden clogs that resemble flip-flops. However, the nanny had none such in her rucksack and resorted to wandering down the street in a cotton dressing gown and her Australian outback boots. I have explained to her that had she requested, the hotel would have lent her a pair. Provided, of course, that she knew the length of her feet in centimetres.

FEBRUARY 26ᵀᴴ, 2000
SIZE MATTERS
Nikkei 225: 19,817

The test tube was too small. Actually, it was a Japanese specimen container, issued by the medical clinic in our building, but, in the opinion of our (non-Japanese) finance director, it was too small.

He had appeared at my desk to complain about his upcoming medical, compulsory company policy on reaching 50. The specimen container was just the first of his objections, which included the barium meal and the anti-spasmodic injection that the clinic was planning to administer. I suggested that he might use an intermediate receptacle to collect the specimen, and then transfer some of it to the test tube.

Actually, this was not the first time that I had heard our finance director complaining about the size of Japanese medical supplies. Previously, the object of his venom was Japanese barrier contraception, which apparently restricted his circulation. This sounded like the ramblings of a fifty-something chartered accountant to me, so I went off to survey the office on the size of Japanese-made condoms.

First stop was my boss, who is American and larger in stature than almost everyone in the office. He told me that when he first came to

55

live in Japan he had to bring in supplies from the US, or purchase them from the American pharmacy in Tokyo. I then checked with the *gaijin* (foreigners) on the trading floor, and they admitted that they also had to source condoms from outside Japan. One Australian salesman, who had come here on exchange as a student, told me that he had purchased three boxes on arrival, and realised that there was a problem the first time that he had had occasion to use one. His immediate response was to call his mother in Sydney and ask her to mail him 10 boxes.

He then disposed of the remaining unwanted items by sending them to each of his friends in Australia, asking them to test them out and give him feedback. The results of this highly subjective survey indicated, I am told, that Japanese-made condoms do not suit Australian sizes.

I have not had to test this theory out for myself, despite the fact that Mr M is Australian. This is because for the first few months after our arrival in Japan I was either pregnant, or (after Number Three's arrival) tired. When I finally started to feel human again, Mr M gallantly offered to have the snip, and did so last summer. We went together to see the consultant the day before the event. "Do you have any concerns?" he asked. "Yes," said my husband. I waited with baited breath. "How long after the operation will I be well enough to play golf?"

The size of the market for condoms is huge in Japan, estimated at some ¥50bn (£281m). The pill was only recently given approval, and it is still not widely used, because of the hassles of getting a prescription.

One of the biggest Japanese condom manufacturers announced this week that it was launching a condom made of polyurethane. When this news appeared on the Bloomberg screen, one of the salesmen remarked that this would be like using a plastic bag. I was more interested in the subsequent paragraphs, which informed me that a line withdrawn in 1998 had been re-launched. Apparently, faults (holes) in the product had been traced to the company's factory – in south-east Asia.

All these imports can't be helping the beleaguered Japanese economy, which is looking like it might be technically back in recession. The well-known reluctance of the Japanese to spend their money is often cited. My observation, for what it is worth, is that they are spending – on imported items. Maybe some enterprising Japanese should set up a condom factory onshore, making larger sizes. This would have the effect of import replacement, an admirable economic goal.

Our economic team tells me Japan does not practice capitalism so much as "social capitalism". Barriers to entry are still widely employed in this country. Even small ones.

MARCH 4TH, 2000
BRUSH WITH THE LAW
Nikkei 225: 19,927

I spent two hours with the police last week. Most people here get no closer to the police than visiting their nearest *koban*. A koban is a Japanese word that translates as "police box"; they are located in every neighbourhood and are usually staffed by a solitary officer.

From this edifice, all manner of information can be obtained, such as where someone lives or who is the registered owner of the bicycle you have found parked outside your house. All bicycles in Japan have to be registered with the police upon purchase. This does not deter illegal parking: the National Census of Illegally Parked Bicycles Near Train Stations is published by the Japanese government and makes for sober reading. Commuters who are irresponsible enough to park their bicycle in the wrong place near the station often come back to find that their transportation has vanished. This, too, was our car's fate after attending a 50th birthday party, and, sadly, we had to go to the proper police station, not the koban. I was the first to be told off, as I had left the house without a handbag and, therefore, was not carrying my alien registration card. This is a piece of plastic the size of a credit card that bears one's photograph, home address in country of origin and other important pieces of information, including one's thumb print. It is compulsory for aliens to carry these upon their person at all times in Japan.

Mr M handed his over instead. There followed much muttering in Japanese, presumably about the Australian propensity to park in the wrong place when attending 50th birthday parties. After what seemed like an age but was probably only half an hour, we were invited to put ¥15,000 (£84) into something that resembled a pay and display machine, and only then were we given a map in Japanese showing us which 24-hour car park our car had been towed to. Maps of Tokyo are hard enough in English; in Japanese, they might as well be blank pieces of paper. In the end, a couple of policewomen took pity and shovelled us into the back of a particularly small police car that was not designed to accommodate two overweight aliens. We were then chauffered to the car park and finally located the missing vehicle. Then disaster struck. Mr M discovered that he was not carrying his correct driving licence. Instead of his Japanese document, he had his English one.

The policewoman lost all sense of humour at this point. Didn't we know that we should carry our Japanese licences at all times? And what was an Australian citizen doing with an English licence, anyway? By this time, it was 2am. Japanese police are armed, so arguing never holds much appeal. Leaving our car overnight was an option, but by the time we returned, the parking charges would have resembled the national debt of a small African country.

I am no stranger to large parking fees. When I gave birth to Son Number Two, I did so at a private maternity hospital in London, frequented by minor royalty and Spice Girls. I went into labour a month early, and as Mr M was overseas, I drove myself there and parked on a single yellow line while I went in for a check. Once we established that I would not be leaving, I asked what would happen to the car. "Don't worry, we'll take care of it," was the answer, and my keys were taken. More than 24 hours later, after Mr M had arrived and inspected his new son, we remembered to ask about the car. "It's in the NCP down the road," was the reply. My caesarean section was covered by the insurance; the parking was not.

We did finally recover our car in Japan. In future, I shall not venture out without my alien registration card, Japanese driving licence, MBA certificate, BA Executive Club card, etc. And I shall travel to all parties by taxi.

MARCH 11ᵀᴴ, 2000
LOVE HOTELS
Nikkei 225: 19,750

The notice under the hairdryer gave it away. In both English and Japanese, it stated: "The hairdryer is only to be used for drying hair."

It was Valentine's Day, and I had taken my husband to a love hotel in Shibuya, an area in Tokyo that has an abundance of these places. A love hotel is a hostelry in which a room can be rented by the hour, with a minimum initial purchase of two hours. There are two rates: one for "rest", which is the lower rate, and the other for "stay", which you can do, for the night, if you check in at 10pm or later.

Of course "rest" is a bit of a misnomer, as the clientele usually do anything but. In a city where the cost of housing means that almost all single people live with their parents until they are married, and many have to do so even afterwards, you're not likely to spend a couple of hours along with your loved one catching up on your beauty sleep.

Mr M met me at 6pm on the day in question and we set off in search of somewhere to check in. In preparation for this expedition, I had canvassed the people in my office, and he had done the same. We had both been told of places with themed rooms, rotating beds, S&M equipment provided in the wardrobes, mirrors on the ceiling and so on. Personally, I didn't mind what it was like, as long as it was clean and had a bathroom with lots of hot water. Mr M, on the other hand, wanted to find somewhere with cable TV that showed the golf channel.

The procedure of checking-in is an experience in itself. The hotel doors are all automatic and spring apart, as though they were expecting you. Inside, there is a deserted reception area without a human being in sight, but an illuminated wall display showing photographs of all the rooms in the hotel. This works on the same basis as a vending machine, the available rooms being lit and the ones taken being dark. Having selected the room that you want to occupy, you press its picture and a ticket appears, which you then take to the check-in desk. This usually has a tiny window so that you cannot see the person taking your money and giving you the key.

For an experience totally devoid of human contact, there's the drive-in love hotel. You drive into an underground garage, select your room, and insert a credit card; your key will then automatically drop into a slot below.

Mr M and I went into some 20 hotels searching for an exotic room, but, after nearly an hour of looking, we settled for one that resembled a motel. Twin microphones were thoughtfully provided for couples who had remembered to pack their karaoke tapes. There were a few cigarette burns in the carpet, but, apart from that it was immaculate, and it had a proper bed rather than a futon.

Across the head of the bed was a control panel from which all manner of things in the room could be activated. These were all labelled in Japanese, but through trial and error we managed to work out what was what. We found the golf channel, after surfing our way through several others, including a few that I assume were pornography. (I say assume, because Japanese TV requires all genitals to be pixelated, as if they were blanking out the faces of people accused of crimes.) We also managed to turn off all the lights, other than a single red spotlight directed on to the bed, and inadvertently raised the room temperature to 30°C.

Modesty forbids much discussion of what actually took place during our hour and 45 minutes, but part of the experience was spending quality time with James Wolfensohn. I managed to locate the BBC World Service on the radio and listen to an entire interview with him on the subject of the World Bank's joint venture with Softbank, that extraordinary Japanese company which is currently trading at over 100 times earnings. Wolfensohn is a compatriot of Mr M's, which is probably why he holds such appeal for me. However, this interview was followed by one with the recently retired IMF head, Michel Camdessus, who I don't find so sexy, so I silenced the radio. There was lots of hot water, and I did enjoy luxuriating in the bath, complete with jacuzzi jets. And I even washed my hair, so I could dry it – with the hairdryer, as instructed.

MARCH 18TH, 2000
WOMEN'S WORK
Nikkei 225: 19,566

As long as you are male, you can work all the hours you like. I suspect that my new human resources manager, a woman, was trying to send me a personal message when she explained that, in Japan, legislation limits the amount of overtime that can be worked by women.

The previous evening we had worked together past midnight, to reconcile the bonus numbers for the office with those issued by head office, write notification letters to 200 people and finalise the payroll. Bonuses are, depending upon your perspective, a blessing or a curse. The theory is that in an industry with such volatile earnings, compensation is most efficiently used as an incentive when linked with results. In good years, shareholders and employees share the rewards. In bad years, the wage bill is kept low. The lack of an upper limit is supposed to act as a strong incentive.

In practice, any investment bank paying out zero bonuses, whatever results it had, is effectively issuing an open invitation to its competitors to poach its staff. With the Nikkei continuing to rise, and good bilingual staff continuing to be in short supply, bonus time is make or break for every investment bank in Japan.

The two of us were engaged in this exercise on the eve of *Hina Matsuri* – literally, "peach blossom" festival. This is a time of celebration for families with young daughters. Originally, they used to make origami dolls and float them down the river as they prayed for health and happiness for their daughters. About 200 years ago, these were replaced by ornate dolls dressed as the emperor, empress and other ceremonial members of the ancient Imperial Household. The dolls are handed down from generation to generation and put on display, like a nativity scene, during the week of the festival. Superstition has it that parents who do not put their dolls away promptly after the festival will have trouble marrying off their daughters.

My nanny, who turns 30 in May, remains unmarried, presumably because they don't have Hina Matsuri dolls in Australia. I am continuing with my efforts to find her a partner. This weekend, she has gone to Beijing; the most handsome and eligible bachelor I know, who works for a European aviation company, is based there, and I have sent him frantic messages via e-mail and voicemail to try and get them together. The dolls might be easier.

With three sons, the nearest thing to a doll in our house is an Action Man. I did stop and look at the doll display in the hotel next to the office, which had some exquisite pieces. It also had an English commentary, which told me that the Hina Matsuri festival was "a celebration of the traditional virtues of Japanese femininity". I have always wondered what those virtues actually were. The pinnacle of achievement for a Japanese wife is to be a *Yamato Nadeshiko*. I once asked a married female Japanese colleague what this meant. Apparently it is "a woman who can understand a Japanese man who has a *Yamato Damashi* (Japanese spirit). A woman who is quiet, patient, supportive, a woman who always behaves in an elegant way (never in a panic) and gracefully, who never ever complains about men's attitudes, even though her husband takes a mistress. A woman who has a real bravery and affection." In other words, a doormat. If those are the traditional virtues of Japanese femininity, they can have them.

One really brave Japanese woman is the newly-elected female governor of Osaka, Japan's second city. The Osaka annual Sumo tournament is about to start, and the winner is presented with their trophy by the governor in the ring. The problem is that the ring, or *dohyo*, is sacred ground, and women are forbidden from setting foot in it. The governor is determined to go ahead; the governing body of sumo has said over its dead body, or an equivalent Japanese phrase. My money's on the men. This is Japan, after all.

The reason why we had to burn the midnight oil over the bonuses was not just because of the tardiness of my instructions from Europe. I was told that the Japanese payroll company needed a full 14 working days to process the payments. They couldn't get it done quicker – they are almost entirely staffed by women. Who can't work the overtime.

MARCH 25ᵀᴴ, 2000
ZERO TOLERANCE
Nikkei 225: 19,958

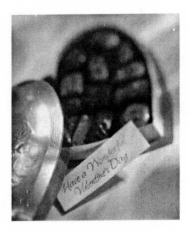

Not one chocolate. Not even a flower. March 14th came and went, and no love token appeared on my desk.

You might be forgiven for thinking that I had my months mixed up. February 14th is Valentine's Day in Japan as well as the rest of the world, but here it is an opportunity for women to give gifts to men, not vice versa. The stronger sex have their turn to show their appreciation a month later, on so-called "White Day".

White Day was invented in 1965 by a confectioner whose principal product was (white) marshmallows. Its purpose was to allow all those men who had received cards or gifts a month earlier to repay the favour, preferably by presenting their lady (or ladies) with a box of sweets. This has the great advantage of reducing the embarrassment factor on Valentine's Day, when receiving a gift from someone that you hadn't sent one to yourself.

Fortunately for those Japanese women who don't like marshmallows, it was quickly adopted by the entire sweet-making industry, and eventually the nation's florists as well. Yet, despite the advertising campaigns announcing the occasion, it seemed to go entirely unnoticed by any of my male employees, or even my husband. His excuse was that it wasn't a UK celebration, so he wasn't going to observe it.

On that basis, I expect great things of him on April 2nd, which is Mothering Sunday in the UK but completely unrecognised in the rest of the world, which celebrates it in May. When I lived in the UK, I usually remembered to buy two cards in March and put one aside to send to my mother-in-law two months later. I would, of course, then lose it and end up sending flowers, because finding a Mother's Day card in May in the UK is next to impossible.

I did remark to my (female, single and Japanese) human resources director that I was rather disappointed with the complete absence of White Day gifts from my employees. She pointed out that I had not actually presented them with any Valentine's Day gifts. I replied that while that may be true, I had just handed over a stack of bonus cheques.

Fortunately, this has signalled the end of a tortuous annual process that begins earlier every year, and is basically an exercise in how to minimise the number of disappointed employees. Calculating bonuses in Japan requires advanced spreadsheet training. The number of zeros involved is so large that I constantly have to reformat the column width, and once you tell the computer to insert the comma that separates the thousands, the problem is compounded even further.

Then I am usually, frantically, scrolling over to the left of the spreadsheet to remind myself of prior year compensation details, since it will not all fit on the same page – unless I either have a two-screen display or reformat the typeface to less than six points (too small to read). Before you all write and tell me how to split the screen while scrolling, let me assure you that I did manage to find someone under 30 to teach me before I got completely frustrated. I now know why my colleagues in Spain and Italy were so delighted to adopt the euro.

The day before White Day, the Japanese government announced that GDP in the fourth quarter of 1999 had fallen, the second quarter in a row that it had done so. This means that Japan is technically back in recession, and ways will have to be found to boost expenditure. There still remains time for everyone in my office (and my husband) to do their bit to increase consumption in the first quarter of 2000 and make up for the poor show on White Day. Between this column appearing and the end of the quarter, it will be my birthday. Make a note – the next GDP figures are due in June.

APRIL 1ST, 2000
FOUR'S A CROWD
Nikkei 225: 20,337

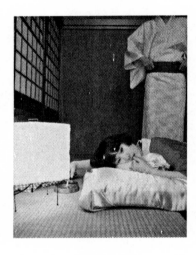

Sex was obviously going to be out of the question. The four futons were immaculate, and all looked very inviting, but they were all in the same room.

Mr M and I, together with another married couple, had driven almost 400 miles from Tokyo to the farthest point of the Noto peninsula, for a child-free weekend away. The hotel, a beautiful traditional *ryokan*, had obviously overestimated just how well we knew each other. No doubt they had also judged that with more than 26 years of marriage between us, sex was going to be the last thing on our minds – either that or we were pure exhibitionists. The husband of the other couple looked crestfallen: their youngest interrupts their sleep most nights and he'd clearly been looking forward to some quality time alone with his wife. The three other bedrooms in the inn were full, so there was no alternative. Tucked up for the night, we resembled my eldest son's school dormitory, if you allow for the fact that the average age there is 10 not 40, and they don't sleep on the floor.

In the past, I have had to share bedrooms with people I knew even less well. The most famous occasion was when a flight I took from Hong

Kong to Australia in 1987 developed a technical fault. All the passengers were sent to a hotel for the night and I discovered that I had been allocated a room with the man sitting next to me, whom I had known for about an hour and with whom I had exchanged all of 10 words before this enforced intimacy. No amount of explanation to the airline at 2am resolved the situation, so, as the room had twin beds separated by a chest of drawers, I agreed to go ahead, provided that the door was propped open with a fire extinguisher. I must have made a reasonable impression on my fellow passenger, as he took me out for dinner when we arrived in Australia and eventually became my husband. I know that this column will appear on April 1st, but I promise you that this is a true account of how I met Mr M.

Back in 1987, I had never slept on a futon. As i have said, a futon in Japan bears no resemblance to those you can buy in the King's Road. Try putting your duvet on the floor, and then get another duvet to sleep under – that will yield the Japanese futon experience. Some of them are not even as thick as an old-fashioned eiderdown, and they certainly don't have wooden slats underneath. Instead, the floor below is usually tatami. It can be jolly uncomfortable, especially if (like Mr M) you sleep on your side, hip bones digging into the floor. I sleep on my tummy, so futons are fine by me.

A *ryokan* could be described as a bed and breakfast, but that is where the comparison ends. Essentially a hotel with two meals, the cost per person is usually well over £100, which my husband regards as an extortionate amount to pay to sleep on the floor and eat dried fish and rice for breakfast. Dinner is served early and in your room, at a low table with cushions around. The correct way to "sit" at this table is actually to kneel, which I can do for three minutes at most. Thereafter, I usually shift from spot to spot, trying to eat and prevent my legs from going to sleep at the same time.

There's no sleeping in, either. A knock on the door at 7am and the screen slides back as a maid enters with a pot of Japanese tea. This is swiftly followed by breakfast (more sitting on the floor), and then you are expected to depart, even if you are returning the same day. Some ryokan do offer western breakfasts of a sort, but we were presented with several pieces of dried fish, brown rice with soy beans, soft-boiled egg with soy sauce (try eating that with chopsticks), and pickled cabbage.

Both couples got to know each other better that first night. They discovered that we snore, and we discovered that they swear violently when woken in the early hours by a cockerel crowing. And, as I had predicted, there was no sex.

APRIL 8ᵀᴴ, 2000
HALF SOAKED
Nikkei 225: 20,252

The broken glass in the bath was the final insult. The management team had trekked 90 minutes out of Tokyo for our twice-yearly, off-site meeting. The whole experience was doomed from the start. My colleague who lives round the corner, the most organised girl in town, slept through her alarm. I sat on my doorstep like an orphan, waiting to share her taxi, and eventually decided to catch my own to the station.

Tokyo's station has two sides. The one that faces the Imperial Palace is a replica of Amsterdam station. The other is a concrete monstrosity. I ran through the building and up the escalator to the platform. Only then did I look at my *shinkansen* (bullet train) ticket and realise that I was not in the "green car", the Japanese version of first class.

My boss, who joined the train at a later station (and in the green car), had selected an amazing venue, a resort built in Italianate style with not a futon in sight. It did, however, have the most beautiful golf course, and, as our meeting extended into the weekend, 18 holes were planned for the next day. Mr M, ever the considerate husband, had volunteered to come up from Tokyo that evening to join the party and take my place on the tee the next day. I had planned to enjoy the resort bath instead.

Having a bath in Japan is unlike anywhere else in the world. The Japanese do not wash in the bath – the purpose of a bath is just to soak away the cares of the world in 40° hot water. Bath etiquette in Japan is

71

clearly understood. Most baths are communal, but the sexes are usually segregated. You enter the changing room and undress, putting your clothes in special baskets and taking the modesty towel provided before moving to the washing area.

The modesty towels are essentially elongated flannels. On the diminutive Japanese female frame, these can (if carefully positioned and held) cover both breasts and what my nanny refers to as her "map of Tasmania". In my case, such coverage is a bit optimistic, so I usually don't bother.

The washing areas have very small, wooden stools that you perch on, and then you use the taps or shower head in front of you to wash carefully all over. You are usually faced by two pump dispensers that contain shower gel and shampoo, although I can never read the labels.

After you are completely clean and no traces of soap or shampoo remain, you can step into the bath. This will be either a large, still bath (*ofuro*), filled up earlier that day, or a bath filled and refilled continuously from a natural hot spring (*onsen*). It may even occasionally be outside: Japan is built on a volcanic range of mountains, and there are more than 2,000 towns and villages where hot springs occur.

I do enjoy lolling around in hot water, although I sometimes wonder whether my body is really suitable for public inspection after three caesarean sections and too much caramel ice cream. After a hard day, I was longing for a soak in the *onsen*. It had been blowing a gale outside, and we had seen the leaves swirling around. So I wasn't surprised when the hotel management came to inform us that the window in the men's *onsen* had broken and that the bath had broken glass in it. I didn't feel that sorry for them – after all, they were all going to play golf the next day.

But then came the killer announcement. As men outnumbered women among other hotel guests, the management had decided to assign the ladies' *onsen* for male use. Ladies could use their en-suite baths to soak in – not the same thing at all. The next morning, we awoke early, if not bright, at 7am, ready to tee-off. I opened the curtains to discover that the whole place was under at least three inches of snow. So much for the golf. That will teach them not to nick my bath.

APRIL 15TH, 2000
SPRING HAS SPRUNG
Nikkei 225: 20,434

Black smoke and pink flowers. The week that Mount Usu erupted in Hokkaido, it was difficult to say which of these natural phenomena was gripping the nation more. The arrival of spring in Japan is most strongly symbolised by cherry blossom, or *sakura*.

The Japanese are obsessed with cherry blossom, and viewing it is a national pastime. There is even a word that translates as "viewing cherry blossom" – *hanami*. People travel for miles to view cherry trees, putting up with terrible traffic jams, punitive motorway tolls and hours in the car just to observe the trees.

Whole families assemble after work at spots in the city where cherry trees are situated, and bring picnics (and alcohol) to share. Leaving the office one day during my first spring in Japan, I remember being asked by one of my Japanese senior managers if I was going *sakura* viewing that night. I looked at him incredulously, thinking of what lay ahead of me – checking homework, searching for teddies, reading bedtime stories, and catching up on reading for my thesis – and wondering why on earth he thought I wanted to go and look at a few trees.

This year, three generations of my husband's family have travelled from Sydney for the event. I am sure they had other motives as well – seeing us, for one thing, and visiting Japan in general, which my mother-in-law has not previously done. A state visit from my mother-in-law is not something to be taken lightly. The morning of her arrival, I was uncharacteristically running around the house checking for dust and sweeping piles of papers and books into drawers in a vain attempt to make the house look marginally less chaotic. I share with numerous other women the sense that I am ever so slightly a disappointment to my mother-in-law. For a start, I am English, and, given that there is no shortage of attractive women in Australia, she might have reasonably expected her son to find a wife at home. Secondly, I have an almost unhealthy obsession with the pursuit of further academic qualifications. Both my sisters-in-law (and, indeed, my husband) have enjoyed incredibly successful careers without needing to bother with a university degree. And, finally, there is no hope of me fitting into any of the clothes that my mother-in-law, an attractive woman with impeccable dress sense, casts off from time to time.

The changing of the season in the natural world has been mirrored, as usual, by the changing of the season in the investment banking world. The bonus season has given way to the resignation season. This is when I lose my voice. Hours and hours of persuading people not to resign from The Bank during the day is followed in the evening by hours and hours of trying to persuade other people to resign from a competitor and join us.

So I have had no time or energy to act as a tour guide from my Australian visitors. My nanny took pity on them and organised several outings, including a visit to Kamakura, a temple-filled seaside town just outside Tokyo that boasts several cherry tree-lined avenues. She drove them down there, a brave move in itself. Parking is usually readily available, if somewhat expensive, and she found a space in an unmanned lot. On returning to the car, she realised that there was no obvious payment mechanism. Having hailed a passer-by and exchanged a few hand signals, she found out where to pay, went in, and asked the man behind the counter to validate the ticket. He spoke English, which was a great relief. "Of course I will validate your ticket," he said. "Which funeral did you attend?"

We live around the corner from one of Tokyo's most famous cemeteries, which is famous for the sweeping lines of cherry trees that run through it, and right now they are all covered with pink flowers.

APRIL 22ND, 2000
UNCONSOLED
Nikkei 225: 18,252

It's pink, plastic and made in Japan. As the Easter holidays are upon us, it has once again appeared in our house. And no, it's not the condom-holder that one of my staff saw fit to purchase for my birthday present. I am talking about the hand-held electronic games console to which my 10-year-old son appears to be addicted.

Japan is the home of electronic games consoles: the best and brightest minds in the world of electronics are to be found here, and even the pages of The Business usually announce at least one new Japanese invention each week. Why they have to apply this genius to electronic games, when it would be far more use in other areas, I don't know.

I am constantly labelled the worst mother in the world for refusing to purchase a console to attach to our television. Ideally, I would ban the telly, but as Mr M works in a TV company, that might be seen as the equivalent of cutting off my Bloomberg access at home.

If we must have a TV in the house, let's use it to watch television, or even videos. What's the point of the BBC spending all this extra money on programming if, when it is finally syndicated to Japan, we use our TV to play games?

Of course, the real money drain is not the console itself. Sony has recently launched its PlayStation 2, which retails in Japan for around ¥40,000 (£325) – if you can lay your hands on one. So far this year, they have shipped 1.3m of these, and my games industry analyst at work tells me that she expects them to ship 10m this year alone. But the purchase price is only just above cost – the key to the money rolling in is the games themselves. On average, each games console owner in Japan purchases six games, compared to three in the EU.

The clamour in my household is not for a PlayStation, because the dreaded Pokémon games will not run on it. For the three or four of you reading this who have not heard of Pokémon, it is a series of electronic games and spin-offs that are based on a rather basic Japanese cartoon series. My views on Pokémon are even stronger than the ones I hold on electronic games, but there's no escaping it in Japan. There is even a Pokémon shop near Tokyo station, where you can buy everything to go with it in every conceivable language.

I have wriggled out of it so far by insisting that a precondition of any purchase is a school report, indicating that an Eton scholarship might not be out of the question. The most recent report was worryingly good, and, even worse, it confirmed that he had been captaining the under-10 rugby B-team, something likely to win him huge amounts of praise from his father. Still, as a colleague pointed out to me, giving in and purchasing would have put paid to any scholarship hopes, anyway.

I didn't voluntarily purchase the dreaded pink plastic handset. It happened when Son Number One and I missed our flight back to the UK after half-term. I was travelling with him because I was heavily pregnant with Number Three, and had run out of time to get back to English-speaking anaesthetists.

Having missed the Virgin flight, I was faced with the stark alternatives of a Japanese delivery room or making my child catch the BA flight with me. Both prospects filled me with terror. BA does not yet have in-seat flight entertainment throughout the plane, and in my household at least, 10-year-old boys fly economy. There are not many things I hate more than these wretched games, but 13 hours with a grumpy and bored 10-year-old is one of them. I gritted my teeth and reached for my wallet. For once, I was going to be the best mother in the world.

APRIL 29ᵀᴴ, 2000
YAKUZA AGM
Nikkei 225: 17,973

One hundred and fifty pounds. I have never caught a cab from Tokyo's Narita Airport to the city, but if I did, that would be the least I could expect to pay. A former boss, on his first visit, wondered why the taxi queue was so short. He soon discovered: if you are less well off than Bill Gates, take the bus or train. If you are Bill Gates, a chauffeured car will meet you. Hence the non-existent queue.

The first-time visitor, whether in taxi, bus or train, is presented with an endless urban sprawl from almost the moment he leaves the airport. The city is very unattractive by day, and also from a distance. The threat of earthquakes means that as much cabling as possible is overground and, combined with a relaxed approach to planning, the whole place looks a mess. Only at street level does the city start to become interesting, with tiny streets and shops, and restaurants located in such obscure places that you wonder how they attract any custom at all.

Whatever the mode of transport to the city, pitfalls for the visitor remain. One of the staff on The Business went to a famous Tokyo department store to purchase some souvenirs. First stop was a headscarf for her grandmother. Having spent a few minutes trying some on, she noticed the embarrassed stare of the shop assistants. She was actually tying around her neck some very expensive *furoshiki*, traditional Japanese wrapping cloths.

Next, she wanted a *yukata,* a cotton dressing gown. On asking for the right department, she received even more shocked and horrified looks because she had used the wrong "y" word and requested the *yakuza* department.

Yakuza are the Japanese equivalent of the Mafia, and you cannot buy one in a department store. They are easily distinguished by an abundance of tattoos and the absence of various fingers above the joint. Apparently, members present their digits to their bosses by way of an apology if they make a mistake. I think this is an excellent idea and should be introduced in my office – it would reduce the number of error reports we have to send to HQ.

I knowingly met my first yakuza the other day at, of all places, a motorway service station. On the way back from a weekend away, Mr M and I stopped for a break. The self-service cafeteria was too much like hard work, so we headed for the table service establishment. It was curiously deserted, and they didn't seem pleased to see us. Nevertheless, we sat down and ordered. After about 10 minutes, a group of Japanese men appeared from around the corner and marched outside, where they got into a black vehicle with darkened windows. The were all dressed as though they were going to a fancy dress party with an Al Capone theme, complete with wide shouldered suits, checked brown fabric and gold chains: textbook gangster fashion. Tattoos and absent fingers were also in evidence. After they had departed, the restaurant began to fill up again – we had obviously interrupted a yakuza AGM, or similar.

At least we avoided the self-service cafeteria. They helpfully put up pictures of the food available above the counter, along with the name of the food (in Kanji) and the price. You then go to a different part of the room, where you put money in a machine and get a ticket, which you exchange for the food. The problem is that the ticket machine has no picture, and my kanji reading is non-existent. I find myself searching for some identifiable pattern in the kanji and then looking for it on the machine, along with the same price as the picture I have selected. Having handed over the ticket, there's a nerve-wracking 10 minutes before the food appears, when I wonder if I am actually going to get what I wanted. When it does arrive, it is always jolly tasty, and at about £2, a much cheaper introduction to Japan than a taxi ride from the airport.

MAY 6ᵀᴴ, 2000
TOY STORIES
Nikkei 225: 18,439

Banned on board. The list of items, 12 in total, that one cannot take on an aeroplane is posted at the security check at Haneda, Tokyo's smaller, domestic, airport. In case the traveller is a foreigner, such as myself, they helpfully provide illustrations of each item on an adjacent board. I noticed the other day that one of these pictures had been replaced with a new one, which looked something like an owl.

On closer inspection, I realised that it was a picture of a Furby. For those of you fortunate enough not to have encountered one, they are soft toys that talk, sleep and talk again, a sort of virtual pet. They are also one of the most annoying things I have ever encountered, and I am not surprised that they are banned on planes. My mother was nearly struck off my Christmas card list for giving one to Son Number One a couple of years ago. The main problem is that they don't have an "off" switch and are likely to talk to you at any time. The only solution is to get hold of a screwdriver and remove the batteries.

I had a Furby-like experience recently. My head trader, the father of two children, has evidently decided that further reproduction is not necessary, and brought a bag of toys to the office for me to pass on to my one-year-old.

I left very late that night and jumped into a taxi, clutching computer, briefcase and said bag of toys. As the bag hit the seat it activated something inside, and the taxi driver and I were subjected to a range of farmyard noises almost all the way home. The language problem meant that I couldn't explain why I was carrying a bag that went "oink" and "moo" every time we turned a corner.

The taxi driver was no doubt unfazed by this – after all, I was a *gaijin* (foreigner). The governor of Tokyo, whose politics closely resemble those of Australia's One Nation party, has warned the police and the army to be prepared for potential riots by foreigners living in the city. I feel like calling him and letting him know that the only thing likely to make me riot is if we have another day when the stock market falls by more than 1,500 points.

I had another worrying experience, while briefly back in the UK the other day. While crawling around on my hands and knees in the temporary Concorde lounge at Heathrow, I met a charming investment banker who worked in a US bulge-bracket firm in London, who was doing the same thing. We were both searching for that elusive airport-lounge phenomenon: a power point where we could charge our telephones and computers.

A little bit later in our conversation, I happened to mention my three children. My companion suddenly asked me if my husband was Australian, something I thought showed either psychic powers or incredible deductive skills, given that I don't wear a wedding ring, let alone one with corks hanging from it. I expressed interest in why he had asked. It turned out that he thought I sounded rather similar to that woman who writes in the FT magazine on Saturdays...

I shall have to start wearing dark glasses or stop flying Concorde. It is rather disconcerting to think that there might possibly be several hundred thousand people who know that I have an Australian husband who plays golf and has had a vasectomy.

That particular trip was memorable for other reasons. It turned out that I was not the only Japanese resident on the flight. The other 11 all held Japanese passports and were thrilled to be travelling on the world's only commercial supersonic jet.

They spent almost the entire three hours and 22 minutes that it took to cross the Atlantic taking photographs of each other in front of the electronic speed display. This seemed to bother me more than it did Lord

Lloyd-Webber or Diana Ross, both of whom were on the flight but are obviously more used to flash bulbs going off continuously inches away from their face. Maybe cameras will have to be added to that list of banned items.

MAY 13TH, 2000
PUBLIC HOLIDAYS
Nikkei 225: 17,357

Shut. Closed. Not open for business. Japan has just been on holiday, and everything ground to a halt. Even the Tokyo American Club, that little piece of the US sitting in the middle of Roppongi, was entirely closed for one day and ran a skeleton service for another two.

Golden Week is the most famous of the three times a year that the Japanese go on vacation. The other two are the New Year and Bon, the festival in mid-August when everyone returns to their home town to honour their ancestors. For me, these three events are similar because they all result in the same thing: complaints from some financial controller 6,000 miles away that the Japanese business has not made budget that month, despite my repeated warnings that January, May and August are going to show lower revenues than other months.

In any investment bank, the manager's year is divided into budget months and bonus months. For me, the former usually run from July to November and the latter from December to April. This leaves May and June as the only two months when managers can take a holiday, which is fantastically inconvenient if, like me, you are blessed with three children.

Golden Week is the name given to the cluster of public holidays that occurs in late April and early May. The first is April 29th. This holiday used to mark the birthday of the previous emperor, who died in early 1989. The new emperor's birthday is December 23rd, which was rather too far away for most people's liking, and, in any case, all the diaries had already been printed. So April 29th stayed a holiday and now celebrates Greenery Day, an opportunity for everyone to appreciate nature. (Mr M usually celebrates Greenery Day by visiting 18 greens, which he feels is entirely appropriate.)

Constitution Day falls on May 3rd, the date that Japan's current constitution was introduced in 1947. May 5th is Children's Day, set aside to pray for the health and happiness of boys and girls. As May 4th was feeling a bit left out, stuck between two public holidays, it was decided to make that a holiday as well – so you can basically write off the week.

If you live in Japan and are planning to go on holiday over Golden Week, about a year's advance planning is required, as the entire country has the same idea. The destinations vary, however. My Single Girlfriend took advantage of the time off last year to nip over to LA for a spot of liposuction and a nose job. A year later, she remains single, so I am not sure if the $10,000 (£6,400) was worth it.

Her destination, a mecca for the film industry, was, ironically, probably the most appropriate for the occasion. Golden Week was a name originally invented by the movie industry in a campaign to get people to go to the cinema in Japan.

They suggested that this string of holidays presented a "golden opportunity" to find time to catch a movie. Over time, the term began to be used to describe this time off from work. Whether they use it to go to the cinema, though, is doubtful. Cinemas are plentiful in Japan, but, like everything else at this time of the year, they tend to be shut.

MAY 20ᵀᴴ, 2000
TEA AND EMPATHY
Nikkei 225: 16,858

Cars are like football. Not just a matter of life and death, but much more important. In Japan, we have been far too worried about the car industry here to notice any of the BMW/Rover/Alchemy/Phoenix carry-on. In a country where well over 80 per cent of households own a car (many of them more than one) and the Toyota badge is a symbol of national pride, the nation is still deep in shock at the fact that three one-time flagships of Japanese car manufacturing are now owned by foreigners.

The first real capitulation was Mazda to Ford. The Japanese comforted themselves with the thought that perhaps this was just a small, niche manufacturer and, therefore, didn't count. Then last year Renault bought a controlling stake in Nissan. At this point, the situation could no longer be ignored. In March, Daimler-Chrysler did the same with Mitsubishi Motors, whose share price had languished as the company had been starved of capital. Essentially, this leaves Honda and the mighty Toyota. The latter is a large and financially strong organisation, likely to remain Japanese for all eternity, but the damage has been done: *gaijin* now run the three companies, unthinkable even five years ago.

The mass hysteria brought on by the passing of motor manufacturing into foreign hands is not new. I am so old that I was part of the team that supported the (unsuccessful) attempt by General Motors to acquire Land Rover in the early 1980s. It didn't matter that the company, through its subsidiary, Vauxhall, had been a substantial contributor to the UK economy for decades. The defence team's portrayal of GM as a predatory foreign company contributed substantially to the failure of the bid.

Nationalistic feelings about car manufacturing are not the only thing that the Japanese have in common with the British. A preoccupation with drinking tea is another. Tea in Japan is a very different product to PG Tips or even Earl Grey. For a start, tea is drunk from cups with no handles, and milk or sugar is never added. Tea bags are readily available in all supermarkets, but restaurants, even the most humble, would not dream of serving anything other than leaf tea. Different teas are served at different stages of the meal, and not all Japanese tea can be described as "green". My own favourite, actually, is brown-rice tea.

Then there is the powdered tea served at tea ceremonies (which looks and tastes like dried pea soup) that is whisked with hot water and then presented to guests. According to custom, they are then supposed to savour its austere taste quietly and serenely. Influenced by Zen Buddhism, the tea ceremony seeks to purify the mind and attain oneness with nature. This is jolly difficult to do when kneeling on tatami, worrying about the fact that the blood has drained from your legs and that incredible pain has started to set in.

Sitting in silence in an uncomfortable position, drinking something that tastes truly hideous, doesn't have much appeal to me. However, it's big business these days. There are schools of tea ceremony, and several of the large hotels having special rooms where (for a fee) you can share the experience of being served tea by a kimono-clad lady.

The hotel next to me has one such room, but I confess that I have not visited it, preferring destinations such as the hairdresser and the bar. The latter I use for interviews with candidates form other banks and the occasional briefing of headhunters, tasks that I find far more congenial with a drink in my hand. Recently, I managed to double-book myself to such an extent that I found myself briefing the headhunter in the hairdresser's instead. The poor man coped nobly with being perched between two Japanese ladies having a manicure, while I dictated the brief with my head in the sink.

The following week we reconvened, not at the office but at the British Embassy. I was getting the documentation to allow me to ship our car back to the UK, and, once again, doing two things at the same time. It remains to be seen whether candidates for the job will arrive with blonde highlights (and not too much off the back, thank you), and the car with a pile of CVs instead of its import papers.

MAY 28TH, 2000@
SAYONARA
Nikkei 225: 16,008

Life is made of ever so many partings, welded together. That is not a translation of a Japanese saying, but a quote from Charles Dickens' *Great Expectations*. It seems apposite for this column, not least because, as I write this, the prime minister who has presided over Japan since June 1998, the month that I arrived, is being cremated in the funeral hall down the road from my house.

Keizo Obuchi had a stroke at the beginning of April and never recovered. It was jolly difficult getting any information on him for the whole time that he lay in a coma. If Tony Blair had been in a coma in a hospital in the UK, the papers would have been covering it daily. The papers here have had no hesitation in reprinting apparently groundless stories about acting prime minister Yoshiro Mori's indiscretions as a student, but showed no interest in covering the plight of the stricken Obuchi. To add to this insult, the forthcoming election has been called for June 25th, Obuchi's birthday. The whole experience has reminded me what a strange country this is.

I, too, am preparing to leave Japan. After nearly two years here, I have been told that it is time to move. This will be my sixth country move in eight years with one bank – another round of inventory compilation, madly trying to guess the worth of our possessions while they lurch from continent to continent in a 40ft container. This time we are even going to ship our car via a roll-on, roll-off service which virtually guarantees that it will arrive at Tilbury without wing mirrors or hub caps.

In some senses, I am relieved to leave. The need to bow to clients and colleagues all the time has meant that I have had to have all my skirts lengthened by six inches, as my legs do not bear close inspection from the rear. Being regularly faced with food that I cannot identify as being animal, vegetable or mineral has become a little wearing. Not being able to use any of my radios because Japan uses a different part of the FM spectrum to anywhere else is another annoyance, while being expected to pay over £1 per courgette means that it's time I got back in touch with reality. Having to smuggle in HIB vaccine to get my baby adequately inoculated because the Japanese do not stock it will be a thing of the past. It will be a relief to live and work somewhere with a street address again, and a two-hour journey to the airport through an unattractive landscape will not be missed.

The buses that tour the city streets blasting out nationalistic music and imperialistic propaganda have been another pet hate. They regularly park outside the gates of the Russian embassy and subject the occupants to abuse over the islands to the far north of Japan, on which not a single Japanese lives but which are the subject of disputed ownership between the two countries. It is no surprise that the other widely-reported story regarding the acting prime minister concerned his comments about Japan's divine nature and imperial heritage. I dread to think what the poor emperor thinks of all this. From all accounts, he is a terribly nice man, with a better-than-average tennis game.

In many other ways I shall be tremendously sad to leave. Japan is a wonderful country, and its people are delightful. Tokyo is a clean, safe and efficient city. My eight-minute commute to work remains the envy of my colleagues in other parts of the world. Cycling to the supermarket, the school or to church with my five-year-old perched on the back will remain a particularly fond memory. Japanese *onsen*, hot spring baths, are one of the most relaxing experiences in the world. The beauty of the changing seasons, the most efficient trains in the world and the simply exquisite cuisine are all things I shall miss tremendously.

It remains for me to thank you for all the letters, invitations and suggestions that you have sent me over the eight months that this column has appeared. Although pressures of work and motherhood have meant that I have not been able to answer each of you, I have appreciated them all. I hope that we shall resume our dialogue again ere long. In the meantime, as they say in Japan, *sayonara*.

CONCLUSION

I returned from Tokyo to work in the United Kingdom in May 2000. It was the absolute peak of the dot.com boom, and the stock market had reached an all time high the month before. I was sad to leave Japan in a way that I have never been sad to leave any other overseas assignment. Going to Japan has been likened by some to the closest experience anyone will ever have of landing on Mars. It is such a distinct culture and way of life that there is nothing else quite like it anywhere in the world.

As I look back, what was I most sad to leave behind? Ask other married women who have lived and raised a family there and their answer might be quite different. As well as my experiences of the place and the people, I was leaving behind more than 200 people who I had looked after like a family for almost two years. Together we had built a business of which we were proud, and which had withstood the dual shocks of the Millennium changeover and the deregulation of commissions.

So when, a year or so later, The Bank decided to shut the whole operation down in a manner that I found quite extraordinary, I went on to write about it again in print. The columns that follow were written when Mrs Moneypenny was back in the UK, had left The Bank and was working elsewhere in her own business. I hope that they show how strongly I felt about my time in Japan and the people with whom I worked.

What would my recommendations be to those of you who have never visited Japan? Perhaps to go there and not do the usual tourist things. Go to the top of the Noto Peninsula, go the furthest reaches of Kyushu, go and ski in Hokkaido, go and see the bits of Japan that the regular tourist route does not take you to. There are the most wonderful places, the most remote locations, and above all the friendliest people. It is a country where one can almost leave one's handbag on a street corner, walk round the block and find it still there when you return with everything inside it. The people are welcoming, hospitable, industrious and generally inspirational. They have some of the best food in the world, the best hotels and the most stunning scenery. They are also people of great innovation who have a fantastic work ethic.

I have nothing but praise for Japan and the Japanese people, despite having been frequently amazed and/or amused by the day-to-day business of living in their country. At the end of this book, I have listed some further reading that those of you who are interested in the subject might enjoy, whether or not you have been there. Japan is somewhere that everybody should experience at least once in their life. I was thrilled to live there, and I would go back there tomorrow.

EPILOGUE

OCTOBER 13ᵀᴴ, 2001
BAD NEWS FROM JAPAN
Nikkei 225: 10,632

Two years of my life were wiped out with a stroke of red pen last week. One hundred and twenty people were made redundant from the bank where I previously worked. Things like this happen regularly, but this time, as they say in the films, it was personal.

Almost without exception, the entire branch had worked for me while I was in Japan. The business I had nurtured, fought for, steered through choppy waters (including two regulatory inspections and the deregulation of stockbroking commissions), was removed from the map. A few people are still there, and The Bank says that it remains committed to Japan (I believe it – how can you be global without being in Japan?) but as far as I am concerned, the guts of the business, essentially my family for a while, has been ripped out.

This can't have been a post-September 11 decision. The Nikkei has been at a 17-year low and Japan is suffering a horrible recession, not helped by the fact that even a reforming prime minister finds it difficult to drive legislation through.

The really extraordinary thing, though, is how I came to hear about it, the day before the actual event. The Japanese office runs a central diary on the computer so that people can see who is marketing what to where. For some reason, the management inserted appointments with outplacement agencies into this planner, and even set aside a time for handling press inquiries. Needless to say, this did not pass unnoticed by the members of staff who happened to log on. They could even read about their departure on Bloomberg before it happened.

At least it gave everyone psychological preparation time, but this is like knowing that someone has a terminal illness. You accept they are going to die, but it is still no less upsetting when it happens.

If you had stepped off the capital-markets planet a year ago and just stepped back on now, it would seem like an entirely different place.

This time last year, as I was working my final weeks in the City, trading volumes were buoyant and talk of recession was just that – talk. How different the picture is now. One of my former protégés at the bank, dating back to my time in Hong Kong, is just going through this surreal experience – a year ago he gave up his job to sail around the world and has arrived back to find that the financial universe has changed.

I am very fond of this particular protégé, although both he and I remember vividly the most awkward conversation I have ever had to have with an employee. Living in a tropical city and working at close quarters with one's colleagues is a fast way to learn the difference in efficacy between antiperspirant and deodorant. I used to lie awake at night wondering how I could suggest to this young man that he might like to use a product that combined the two. In the end, I waited until his birthday, then bought him the most expensive shirt I could find – and presented it to him together with a suitable product that I assured him would be the best way to avoid ruining such a superb garment.

I then gently pointed out that, while he was possessed of a first-class brain and exemplary social skills, excess perspiration might occasionally detract from these exceptional qualities.

This must have made an impression – in the promotional material for the company arranging his voyage, he states that his must-pack item was a deodorant (hopefully combined with an antiperspirant!). I was delighted when, towards the end of the race, I received an e-mail telling me that he had fallen in love with a crew-member from another boat, and that she apparently returned his affections – despite the fact that the deodorant, although originally packed, had long since run out. He is now back on dry land, and I am pleased to report that (a) he has been to the chemist to stock up and (b) his girlfriend is still very much in evidence.

I had once thought him as a suitable escort for my nanny, whom several of you have written recently to ask about. Sadly, a relationship with the teacher, which had looked so promising, came to naught; he pitched up at the airport upon our return from Australia, clutching flowers and having prepared a candle-lit dinner, but 24 hours later he called to say it was all a terrible mistake and he wasn't ready for a girlfriend. You can imagine that he is no longer among my favourite people. Neither, of course, are those whose decision put 120 of my former colleagues out of work last week.

NOVEMBER 3RD, 2001
DOWNSIZING, RUBBER GLOVES AND BANKERS
Nikkei 225: 10,383

Anniversaries are useful prompts. One year ago I left the sheltered and privileged world of a glass-fronted air-conditioned office in London EC2 and started work in a room shared by three others where the only ventilation is a window. This, when opened, ensures that anything on my desk immediately relocates to the floor.

Do I regret it? No. Am I richer? In monetary terms, most definitely not. In lifestyle terms, most definitely yes. I have learnt many things along the way. One is that you cannot change the way a company is run overnight, especially if it has been going for 20 years before you even showed up. My long campaign to buy a dishwasher was testimony to that – I am delighted to tell you that one has finally arrived. Tired of endless debate and no action, I purchased a dishwasher from the website of a well-known electrical retailer for £155 and had it delivered while my partners were on holiday. Only then did I discover what re-plumbing had to go on to accommodate it, which cost twice as much as the appliance itself. Still, we have another three years of our lease over which to write off the installation costs, and the machine itself will move with us to the next office.

The arrival of the dishwasher has come as welcome relief for our staff, one of whom has even started to paint her nails again now she doesn't have to don yellow rubber gloves each day.

I am not sure if my colleagues look a year older than when I joined; personally I feel at least a year younger. The economic slowdown (we are still not technically in recession) has certainly affected us. However, here I feel that my own efforts might be able to directly affect our performance, whereas my toils as one of the 100,000 employees of my previous employer were as drops in the ocean.

When I shared with you recently my sadness in having my hard work in Japan dismantled, several of you wrote to me with your views. One or two of you came from the "why shed tears over the demise of another few bankers, they're all rich and overpaid anyway" school of thought, and I do have some sympathy with this. Many of those who are losing their jobs now in the Square Mile have been overpaid for years and if they have been prudent with their money will not be facing severe hardship. The high salaries and bonuses enjoyed by many investment bankers are high because there is no job security; many of them conveniently forget that. My sadness was more over my own sweat and tears, for which I was not uncommonly well paid (remember that I'm a woman), and also for the manner in which they were dismissed. Virtually all of them were Japanese and working in Tokyo, where it is hard enough to recruit for a foreign bank precisely because they have a reputation for downsizing savagely with little consideration. In Japan, culture dictates that (unless you are being dismissed for disciplinary reasons) you should at least be allowed to e-mail all your contacts and clients to alert them of your departure; this was effectively denied to my former colleagues. Japan is not a country in which to start a business lightly; regulators, and people in general, have long memories.

Others of you recognised that this was the inevitable result of the usual management decision to put people who have no management skills in positions of authority, simply because they are good at their existing job. It does not follow that if someone is good at structuring complex financial transactions, they will also be good at managing people. As a manager who has made those difficult decisions myself, I confess that it isn't easy. If you have two people up for promotion, one with better finance skills than the other, who has better management skills, you are still almost always going to promote the former because he or she will command the respect of their peers. If you promote the better manager, the chances are that your best fee-earner will walk out of the door. I learnt many things at business school, but this was one dilemma they never prepared me for.

No wonder I swapped a global banking operation for a tiny little company in London W1. One thing I do miss, I confess, is my ergonomically designed swivel chair (3,000 of them purchased when the bank's UK staff moved into their new offices a couple of years ago), but I am hoping that someone might manage to buy me one when I am 40 next spring. That's another anniversary that is going to act as a useful prompt.

RECOMMENDED READING

This represents a very personal selection, as you can obviously find many books on Japan in both general and specialist bookshops. One specialist bookshop in London on Japanese books is the Japan Centre Bookshop at 212 Piccadilly, tel: 020 7439 8035.

Robert J. Collins, *Max Danger: The Adventures of an Expat in Tokyo,* 1987, Charles E. Tuttle (we are not sure if this is still in print).

Max Danger: The Continuing Adventures of an Expat in Tokyo, 1988, Charles E. Tuttle (still in print)

This is a collection of columns, written by a fictitious character, Max Danger, a US expatriate living in Tokyo with a US expatriate wife. Robert Collins, the author, is American but has a Japanese wife in real life.

Bill Emmott, *The Sun Also Sets: Limits to Japan's Economic Power,* 1989 by a number of different publishers.

I am an unashamed Bill Emmott fan and have been ever since I read this book. He has written many more books since, but this one provides a unique insight into the Japanese "economic miracle" and should be compulsory reading for anyone thinking of going to live or work in Japan.

Richard McGregor, *Japan Swings: Politics, Culture and Sex in the New Japan,* 1996, Allen & Unwin

This book, more than any other, gives a real insight into some of the more bizarre activities that go on in Tokyo. The author, now the FT correspondent in Beijing, is Australian and worked for a long time for the Australian press. Despite the surname, we are not related, have never met, and this is not the Australian Mr McGregor that I married! Nonetheless, if you can get hold of a copy of this book, it is truly fascinating.

Gillian Tett, *Saving the Sun***,** 2004, Random House Business Books

Gillian Tett also works for the FT, and was stationed in Japan for a long time. This is a book in the tradition of *Barbarians at the Gate* (KKR's takeover of RJR Nabisco) and *Conspiracy of Fools* (the demise of Enron), in other words books about large capital markets transactions and corporations, written in such a human and personal way that it feels more at times as if you are reading a novel. The account of the Ripplewood acquisition of LTCB, one of the largest banks in Japan, *Saving the Sun* shows how Japan has become part of the global capital market and how things have changed enormously over the past twenty years. Despite the subject matter, highly readable.

Printed in the United Kingdom
by Lightning Source UK Ltd.
115617UKS00001B/91-144